FREDDY VS SCHOOL

by NEILL CAMERON

FREDDY VS SCHOOL

by NEILL CAMERON

David Fickling Books

Scholastic Inc. / New York

With special thanks to Anthony Hinton and Katie Bennett

AW YEAH!

BOOM!

Copyright © 2021 by Neill Cameron

All rights reserved. Published by Scholastic Inc., *Publishers since 1920*, by arrangement with David Fickling Books, Oxford, England. SCHOLASTIC and associated logos are trademarks and/or registered trademarks of Scholastic Inc. DAVID FICKLING BOOKS and associated logos are trademarks and/or registered trademarks of David Fickling Books.

First published in the United Kingdom in 2021 by David Fickling Books, 31 Beaumont Street, Oxford OX1 2NP. *www.davidficklingbooks.com*

The publisher does not have any control over and does not assume any responsibility for author or third-party websites or their content.

COPYRIGHT INFORMATION!

So FASCINATING!

Library of Congress Cataloging-in-Publication Data available

ISBN 978-1-338-68681-4

1 2021

Printed in the U.S.A.   23
First printing, 2021

FOR
LOGAN!

Okay, humans, listen up! Here are the . . .

TOP 5 THINGS YOU SHOULD PROBABLY KNOW ABOUT ME!

1. My name is **FREDDY**.

2. I live in London with my mom and dad.

3. I go to school.

4. I have a big brother named Alex.

5. Oh yeah, the **MAIN** thing: I am an

AWESOME ROBOT!

. . . I should maybe have started with that?

I have many **AMAZING ROBOTIC ABILITIES**.

I can . . .

FLY!

FWOOSH!!

And also I have

LASERS!

KZOW!

KZOW!

And also I am **SUPER STRONG** and I can **LIFT REALLY HEAVY STUFF** and also *PUNCH* BUILDINGS SO HARD THEY FALL OVER, and stuff like that.

The only thing that stinks, though, is that I am hardly ever allowed to actually **DO** any of this stuff.

I am only supposed to **FLY** or use my **LASERS** and stuff "under strictly supervised conditions" at my mom's work. Not at home, not in the street. And definitely not at school.

Which is why everyone got so annoyed just because I flew through the staff-room window **ONE TIME**.

Anyway, that . . .

KRASH!!

. . . that was how everything started.

CHAPTER

My mom has had to come into school to have meetings about me lots of times. Like, **LOTS** of times. And the thing that annoys me is, not **ONCE** has it been about anything good. It's never "Oh, hey, we just wanted to tell you that Freddy is really awesome and is doing great in school." Oh no. It's always "We regret to inform you that Freddy has accidentally destroyed **THIS** or set *FIRE* to **THAT** or exploded **SOMETHING ELSE** with *LASERS*."

THIS time, Mr. Javid—he's the vice principal—was all:

MRS. SHARMA... And Mom was like:

IT'S DOCTOR SHARMA.

And he didn't like that, either.

So he was all: "Doctor Sharma, I'm sure you appreciate that . . . incidents like this put the school in a very difficult position . . . We have tried to be sensitive to your children's, uh . . . particular needs . . . But we have to think of the other pupils . . ."

And just kind of . . .

...BLAH BLAH BLAH BLAH BLAH...

. . . generally.

I did try to EXPLAIN what had happened . . .

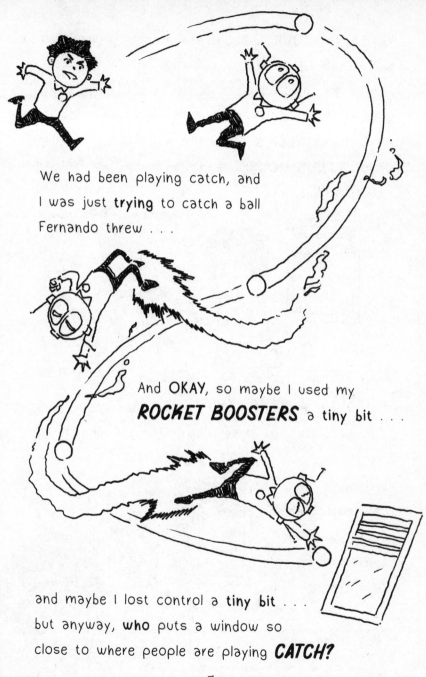

We had been playing catch, and
I was just **trying** to catch a ball
Fernando threw . . .

And **OKAY**, so maybe I used my
ROCKET BOOSTERS a tiny bit . . .

and maybe I lost control a **tiny bit** . . .
but anyway, **who** puts a window so
close to where people are playing ***CATCH?***

Anyway, of **COURSE** it turned out that the window I accidentally flew through was the one in the staff room. The teachers were all sitting around in there drinking coffee and, I dunno, doing whatever teachers do in there. They are all quite old, so . . . talking about **BUYING HOUSES** and how much their **BACKS HURT**, probably?

YES.
HOUSES.

SO EXPENSIVE.

MY SPINE!

Then I came **CRASHING** through the glass, and our class teacher Miss Obasi jumped like three feet in the air and spilled her coffee all over the carpet and had to be taken off for a Nice Quiet Nap.

"Freddy," said Mom, "you know you're not supposed to use your **ROCKET BOOSTERS** at school."

"I know," I said. "But we were playing, and I forgot. I was just—"

"Showing off?" she asked.

"I wasn't showing off!" I protested. Although **YES**, okay, I totally had been showing off.

"The point," said Mr. Javid, "is that we cannot afford to have any more incidents like this. And therefore, starting this semester, we will be requiring Freddy to sign up to a new **CODE OF CONDUCT** . . ."

Then he pulled out this piece of paper that he clearly had all ready to go, with printed on it in **BIG BOLD LETTERS** . . .

ROBOTIC CODE OF CONDUCT

USE OF SUPERHUMAN ROBOTIC ABILITIES IS STRICTLY FORBIDDEN ON SCHOOL GROUNDS.

NO SUPER-STRENGTH

NO LASERS

NO ROCKET BOOSTERS

As I am the only one in our year who even **HAS** **SUPER-STRENGTH** or **LASERS** or **ROCKET BOOSTERS**, this seemed **SUPER UNFAIR** and also possibly discrimination? But Mom just sighed, and said she wished she'd never told me about discrimination, and promised Mr. Javid there wouldn't be any more incidents.

". . . will there, Freddy?" she said.

"No! I can be good!" I said. And then, because I felt like I should be honest here, I added, "I mean, I'll try."

But Mr. Javid wasn't having it. He was all: "I'm afraid 'try' isn't going to be enough. We are implementing a strict three strikes policy with regard to the **CODE OF CONDUCT.**"

"Three strikes!" Which actually sounded kind of cool, like having lives in a video game or something.

LIVES:

So **THEN** I started daydreaming about there being an awesome video game about **ME** and my adventures . . .

"Freddy!" my mom said, sounding angry. "Are you even listening?"

"Yes!" I said. Although **FINE**, okay, I totally hadn't been listening. "So, wait, what happens if I use up my three lives? Do I, like, start again, or . . . ?"

"As I just explained," said Mr. Javid, looking **PARTICULARLY** annoyed, "if you break the rules three times, you will be . . .

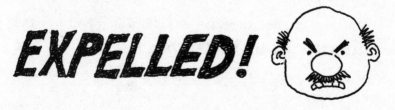

CHAPTER

ROBOTIC CODE OF CONDUCT

USE OF SUPERHUMAN ROBOTIC ABILITIES IS
STRICTLY FORBIDDEN ON SCHOOL GROUNDS.

NO SUPER-STRENGTH

NO LASERS

NO ROCKET BOOSTERS

On Monday, at recess, me and Fernando were
standing outside the cafeteria. Mr. Javid had put the
ROBOTIC CODE OF CONDUCT up on the wall
in massive letters for everyone to see, and people

kept walking past and giggling and pointing, and it was **TOTALLY CLEAR** they were all talking about me.

Normally I LIKE people talking about me. Because I am an **AWESOME ROBOT** and everyone else at my school is **NOT**, people are always very interested in seeing me do cool tricks with my **LASERS** and **ROCKET BOOSTERS** and stuff. It is fun. It is like being a . . .

But if I haven't done anything like that, and everyone is talking about me, anyway . . . then I don't know **what** they're saying.

And that doesn't feel so fun.

"Stinks about that sign," said Fernando.

FERNANDO

Fernando is my Best Friend (Human). He is always saying things like:

GO ON,
DO IT! —

DO IT! —

DO ⁓
//////T!

On the very first day I started school, he came up and said, "You are a robot. That is **AWESOME**," and I **AGREED**, and he has officially been my Best Friend (Human) ever since.

"It **DOES** stink about that sign," I agreed. "It's like they made up special rules just to stop me being able to do anything **FUN**."

"Hey," said Fernando, "at least we've still got **THIS**." And he rolled up his sleeve and pointed to the **Secret Robo-Communicator Watch**.

This is an **Awesome** and **Highly Technological Device** that my mom made and that I gave to Fernando. The way it works is, he can call me on it and I will see him on, like, a screen in my head. And it works wherever we both are!

COME IN, FREDDY! OVER!

I READ YOU! OVER!

"Come on," said Fernando. "We can play Security Officers. It'll be fun! What else are you going to do, stand there sulking all day?"

So I agreed, and Fernando ran off across the playground. Security Officers is a thing we do where we split up and sneak around the school looking for TROUBLE, and then call each other on the watch to report whatever we find.

Okay, **BASICALLY** it is spying on people. It is pretty fun! Fernando is very good at coming up with games. It is literally like the one fun thing about school.

I asked my mom once why we even have to **GO** to school. Most **ROBOTS** don't have to go to school. They get to do awesome stuff like **BUILD CARS** or

PUT OUT *FIRES* or OPERATE IN *DANGEROUS* OVERSEAS WAR ZONES.

I could do any of those things! I would be **AMAZING** at operating in **DANGEROUS** OVERSEAS WAR ZONES.

But nooooo, I have to go to school, just because I am sentient. In fact, me and my big brother, Alex, are the **ONLY** sentient robots in the WHOLE WORLD.

This is, for some reason, a super-big deal, even though I am not exactly sure what it actually means.

I asked my mom, and she said, "It means . . . you have a mind. You're self-aware. You're a person."

Anyway, apparently being sentient means you have to go to school, so, frankly, you can keep it.

Here are my . . .

 **WORST THINGS ABOUT SCHOOL**

1 You have to go there every day. **EVERY DAY!**

2 You have to wear boring clothes that look the same as everyone else's.

3 You have to spend all day doing math.

4 MATH.

5 MATH.

I swear, it is basically **MATH JAIL**. I have no idea how any of this is even legal.

It is particularly frustrating because, as I have mentioned, I am an **AWESOME ROBOT!** Like, my brain is literally a computer. I could just use the **calculator app** in my head and get everything right all the time, but nooooo.

My mom says it's really important for me to learn everything "the human way." Which seems **POINTLESS**, but "those are the rules," apparently, and "no amount of threatening to **BLOW** everything up with **LASERS** is going to change them."

Suddenly my antennae started pinging. It was the **Secret Robo-Communicator Watch!**

BOOP BOOP!

I answered the signal, and Fernando popped up on my screen, shouting, "Freddy! I found some trouble going on! **BAD** Trouble! We're over by the garbage cans—get over here!"

I was just getting ready to MEGA ROBO POWER UP and fire up my *ROCKET BOOSTERS* to fly over there . . .

WVRRMM

. . . when I looked up and saw . . .

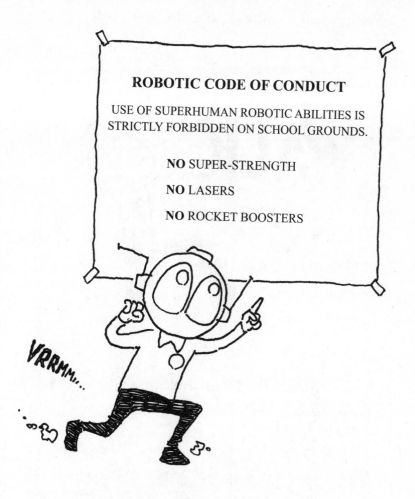

ROBOTIC CODE OF CONDUCT

USE OF SUPERHUMAN ROBOTIC ABILITIES IS
STRICTLY FORBIDDEN ON SCHOOL GROUNDS.

NO SUPER-STRENGTH

NO LASERS

NO ROCKET BOOSTERS

VRRMM...

The sign. The **CODE OF CONDUCT**, right there on the wall. Saying that ***ROCKET BOOSTERS*** were **STRICTLY FORBIDDEN**. Which meant . . . **NO** ***FLYING*** allowed.

Which meant . . . I had to walk over there.

I hate walking, it is **SO BORING**, I don't know how humans manage it.

As I walked across the playground, I realized that this was what it was going to be like now, not being allowed to use my ***ROCKET BOOSTERS*** or ***LASERS*** or anything. Being an ***AWESOME ROBOT*** celebrity was, like, the one thing that made school fun, and I wouldn't be one anymore. I would just be a . . . regular person.

Except not a regular person. I'd still be a robot. So I'd get all of the pointing and whispering, but none of the fun stuff.

REGULAR PERSON ↘

WHISPER!

POINT!

STARE!

Basically I did not like the thought of this at all.

"What took you so long?" asked Fernando when I finally arrived. "Didn't you hear me say there was **BAD TROUBLE?**"

"Don't blame me!" I said. "Blame the stupid **CODE OF CONDUCT!**"

"Look!" said Fernando. A bunch of kids were standing around the bike sheds, and it looked like they were centred around . . .

Uh-oh . . . Henrik.

CHAPTER 3

HENRIK

Henrik is in our class. He is . . .

- TWICE AS **BIG** AS ALL THE OTHER KIDS FOR SOME REASON?

- SEEMS **ANGRY** A LOT.

- YOU DO **NOT** WANT TO GET ON THE WRONG SIDE OF HIM, BASICALLY.

Fernando told me how back in, like, first and second grade, before I started at school, he would always do things like just **FLIP OUT** or **THROW CHAIRS AROUND** or **BEAT PEOPLE UP FOR NO REASON**. He was always having to go and have meetings with Mr. Javid—even more than **ME**.

Fernando said he heard one of the teachers say that if Henrik beat up one more person he might get **EXPELLED**, or even "Taken Out of Mainstream Education" altogether, whatever **THAT** means.

So, of course, everyone was basically terrified of Henrik because of his **MASSIVENESS**, and also all the chair throwing and stuff.

Anyway, then I came along and, as I possibly mentioned, I am an ***AWESOME ROBOT*** and I have

LASERS and am **BASICALLY INDESTRUCTIBLE** and stuff. So I wasn't scared of Henrik, and then Fernando decided he wasn't scared of Henrik, either, and me and Fernando formed, like, an **ANTI-HENRIK LEAGUE** together. And Henrik didn't like that AT ALL, so basically ever since I started school he has totally had it out for me.

He is always making rude comments at me, and calling me *"ROBOT"* instead of my name, and tripping me in P.E. and stuff. Frankly I think I have been very good about it, because I have not shot him with lasers, not even **ONCE**. But does anyone say "Well done, Freddy" because of this? **THEY DO NOT**.

"Check it out," said Fernando. "Henrik's gone **FULL HENRIK** on the new kid."

New kid

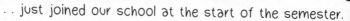

... just joined our school at the start of the semester.

- I THINK HIS NAME IS **RIYAD**?

- I HAVEN'T REALLY TALKED TO HIM MUCH, TO BE HONEST.

- HE SEEMS... **SMALL** AND **NERVOUS**?

Anyway, today it looked like Henrik had stolen this Riyad kid's lunchbox.

Even though we are all in the same grade, Riyad is literally, like, half Henrik's size, so Henrik was holding the lunchbox up over him so he couldn't reach it. And as for the lunchbox . . . Oh man.

It was bright pink and had unicorns on it, from this show **MAGIC UNICORN SQUAD,** which is for little kids. So Riyad really wasn't helping himself there, because everyone knows that liking stuff that is for little kids is one of the **Things You Just Don't Do.**

It looked like Riyad was starting to get upset. Which is another **Thing You Just Don't Do.**

Riyad said, "Please, I need it, put it down."

"I'm just having a look," said Henrik. "Why's it got unicorns on it? Are you a baby?"

And some other kids laughed. And Riyad looked super embarrassed and just said, really quietly, "My mom bought it."

Which was maybe the wrong thing to say to Henrik, because apparently he found that hilarious.

"Awww," he said, doing, like, a silly baby voice. "Mommy bought it. Is you mommy's wittle baby?"

And he gave Riyad a big shove so he fell down on the pavement. And now Riyad looked like he was going to start crying. Which is like the all-time Number One **Thing You Just Don't Do**. And that just got Henrik going even more.

"Awwww," said Henrik, still doing the baby voice. "Is mommy's wittle baby going to cwy?"

Riyad just sat there, staring at the ground, and said, really quietly, "It's new. Please."

Henrik did this big sneery grin and said, "Baby wants it back? Baby go get it."

And he **THREW** Riyad's unicorn lunchbox, right up onto the roof of the bike sheds!

Henrik was laughing, and some other kids were laughing, and Riyad just sat there on the ground looking really upset and, basically, I had had about enough of this. If there is one thing I do not like . . . it is **INJUSTICE**.

I wanted to help the new kid. And with my ***ROCKET BOOSTERS,*** it would be so **EASY** to help. But it said right there in the **CODE OF CONDUCT: NO ROCKET BOOSTERS.**

But then I thought, the whole reason they had the stupid **CODE OF CONDUCT** was to stop me "showing off." But this wouldn't BE for showing off. This would be for **FIGHTING INJUSTICE**. Which was like a whole different thing.

SHOWING OFF ✗

FIGHTING INJUSTICE ✓

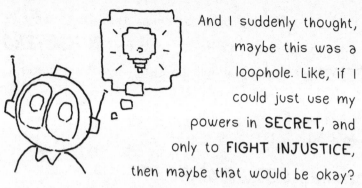

And I suddenly thought, maybe this was a loophole. Like, if I could just use my powers in **SECRET**, and only to **FIGHT INJUSTICE**, then maybe that would be okay?

It would be like I was an awesome . . .

which is maybe even better than being a celebrity. But, also, it is a **SECRET**.

And anyway, **EVEN IF** I did get caught, I'd still have two strikes left, and that's **LOADS**.

I quickly looked around to check that there weren't any teachers around, so that my **SUPERHERO SECRET** Identity would be safe. And there weren't, so it was.

And so I . . .

MEGA ROBO POWERED UP!

CHAPTER 4

It was, basically, **TOTALLY AMAZING**. It was honestly like something out of a movie. I **FIRED UP** my **ROCKET BOOSTERS**, and I **FLEW** right up over the bike sheds, and I **GRABBED** Riyad's lunchbox, and I **CAME RIGHT BACK DOWN** before any of the teachers saw.

Basically my first Secret Superhero Mission was a . . .

TOTAL SUCCESS!

Woo!

YEAH!

"That was awesome," said Fernando. I **AGREED**.

"What's going on?" asked my other friend Anisha, who had just wandered over to see what was going on.

ANISHA

Anisha is my other Best Friend (Human), even though when me and Fernando are coming up with FUN PLANS, she will often say stuff like . . .

THIS IS
WEIRD. —

THIS IS
POINTLESS. —

THIS IS
WEIRD AND —
POINTLESS.

. . . and go off to play field hockey instead. Field hockey! **LITERALLY THE MOST WEIRD AND POINTLESS GAME EVER INVENTED.**

"Freddy," said Anisha, "I thought you weren't supposed to use your powers at school?"

"It's fine!" I said.

"Like, I could have sworn they literally just put up a big sign about this,"
continued Anisha.

"It's **FINE!**" I repeated.
"I am **FIGHTING INJUSTICE!**"

And then I double-checked that no teachers were around to see what I'd done, but they weren't, so it was **FINE**.

I walked over to Riyad and handed him his lunchbox, and there was actual clapping and cheering from all the kids standing around watching. Riyad literally hugged his lunchbox, he was so happy to have it back.

Henrik . . .

. . . was less happy.

"Think you're so smart, don't you, Robot?" he said, giving me a shove. "How about I go tell on you to Javid for flying, huh? Bet you might get in a bit of trouble for that."

"Do it," I said. "But then maybe I'll tell on **YOU** for how you were picking on the new kid? I bet you might get in trouble for THAT."

It was like a tense, exciting . . .

Except that everybody knew that no one was really going to tell on anyone to the teachers, because that is another **Thing You Just Don't Do**. I mean, not as bad as liking stuff that is for little kids or crying. But still, pretty bad.

"Hit him!" someone yelled to Henrik, unhelpfully.

"If you hit him, I'll hit **YOU**," said Fernando.

"Nobody needs to hit anybody," said Anisha, and then muttered something in Punjabi, which, thanks to my onboard translation software, turned out to mean a very rude word, and then ". . . boys."

"Fine," said Henrik. "No hitting. I've got a better idea."

And he grinned and got a look in his eye that I can only describe as an actual **EVIL GLEAM**.

EVIL GLEAM!

"Let's settle this."

"Settle this how?" I asked.

THROWING CONTEST!

he said.

"Human versus Robot. Let's see who's strongest, once and for all. Unless you're too **CHICKEN**."

And he did this big smug grin. Henrik can be **SO ANNOYING**. It's like he thinks just because he's bigger and stronger than everyone, that means he can do what he wants. And that is literally, like, the definition of **INJUSTICE**.

Which, as I mentioned, I am **NOT INTO**.

"Do it, Freddy!" said Fernando. "Teach this guy a **LESSON!**"

"You're on," I said. "What are we throwing?"

Henrik grabbed the lunchbox back from Riyad, who was still standing there. "Unicorn lunchbox," he said.

GRAB!

Riyad looked a bit alarmed by this.

"It's fine, don't worry," I said to him. "I'll get it right back to you. We just need to teach this guy a lesson. About **JUSTICE**, and about not picking on people, and about who is **ACTUALLY STRONGEST**. Okay?"

"Um," said Riyad. Which I assumed probably meant yes.

So we all went over to the edge of the school field, and everyone lined up, and Henrik stepped up to take the first throw.

"Stand back, everyone," he said.

FOR **JUSTICE!**

Um.

...WATCH **THIS!**

And he sort of
spun his arm
around and around,
like one of those
guys on the
Olympics doing
the hammer throw,
or the shot put,
or whichever
one it is.

The lunchbox was just a **BLUR OF PINK**.
And then he let go, and . . .

. . . . it sailed out over the
field, coming down with a . . .

THUNK!

halfway up the soccer field.

There was some clapping and some cheering and even a couple of **WHOOPs**. Henrik did his biggest smuggest grin and said, "Beat THAT, Robot."

Anisha sent someone off to retrieve the unicorn lunchbox, and Fernando went to stand where it had landed as a marker.

"Do it, Freddy!" shouted Fernando, from up the field. "Show him!"

I double-checked that there weren't any teachers out on the field, but it was okay, we had the all clear. So I decided to really teach Henrik a lesson, and give everyone a show, and use my **SUPER ROBOT STRENGTH** to throw this sucker . . .

...TO THE FLIPPING MOON!

Everyone was clapping and cheering and yelling **"FREDD-Y! FREDD-Y!"** and I decided that being a superhero was definitely **EVEN BETTER** than being a celebrity.

So I did just like Henrik had, and spun around and around with it, until the lunchbox was like a **PINK TORNADO**, and then just as I was about to throw it . . .

DISTRACTION!!

I completely lost my grip and the lunchbox flew out of my hand backward, going incredibly fast, right toward . . .

. . . Miss Obasi. Who was walking across the playground, holding a cup of coffee.

"Look out!" someone yelled, but it was too late. The lunchbox **CRASHED** into her coffee cup, sending it flying, and then the mug and the lunchbox hit the ground, both of them smashing apart into tiny pieces with a massive . . .

SMASH!

Miss Obasi gave this bizarre sounding noise, sort of a **GYEAAARGGHH**, and jumped like three feet in the air.

Just then, my big brother, Alex, came walking around the corner of the playground and saw the whole scene.

Pieces of broken mug and pink plastic and spilled coffee, and bits of Riyad's lunch, **SPRAYED** all over the playground. And Miss Obasi standing there clutching her chest and shaking like she'd just had a **HEART ATTACK**. And everyone standing around staring at me.

And without even slowing down, Alex just said, "Nope," and turned around, and walked back around the corner.

Alex is not very helpful sometimes.

Mr. Javid came charging out of the school huffing and puffing. He ran over to Miss Obasi to check she was all right. And then, without even asking anyone what had happened or who had done it, he looked over, glaring. Right at me. And he said:

FREDDY. SHARMA.

Just assuming it was me that had done it.

I mean, yes, okay, it was actually me that had done it.

But it is not nice to assume.

CHAPTER 5

"I'm not angry, I'm just disappointed," Mom said to me on the Skytube home, after she'd had to come in to school for yet another meeting, this time about the Lunchbox Incident. But it sounded like she actually was angry, and I pointed this out.

"Okay, yes! Fine! I am angry **AND** disappointed!" Mom said, **QUITE LOUDLY**. But then everyone in the car started looking around, so she went back to using her quiet voice.

"Everything we talked about . . . you promised me you'd try. And now that's your first strike, and you're just two more incidents away from being expelled. And how long did you last?"

I was about to answer, but then I realized that this was probably a trap, because she actually knew the answer already.

"One day," she said.

"It wasn't my fault!" I protested. "I was **FIGHTING INJUSTICE!**"

"You broke some poor boy's lunchbox. You almost gave your teacher a heart attack. What part of that, exactly, is 'fighting injustice'?"

And when she put it like that, I had to admit it didn't sound very good. I was pretty sure I had been fighting injustice, but then everything got . . . confused.

We sat in silence the rest of the way.

When we got home, Mom went into her lab and was banging things around even louder than usual, and through the door we could hear occasional bits of **EXCITED SWEARING**.

MOM

My mom works at a place called **R.A.I.D.**, which stands for Robotics . . . Analysis . . . Inter . . .?

Okay, look, I can't actually remember what it stands for. Anyway, the point is, she is a **BRILLIANT INVENTOR** and **CYBERNETISIS** . . .

CYBERNITISUS . . .

CYBERNOTIS . . .

. . . she is a **ROBOT SCIENTIST**.

My mom is always saying things like:

FREDDY, STOP DOING THAT. —

FREDDY, STOP — DOING **THAT** ALSO.

FREDDY, — **NO!**

Even though my mom is an amazing robot scientist, she did not actually build me and Alex. We are adopted, which means she is our mom, even though she did not build us.

DAD

My dad is not a genius scientist or robot inventor or anything. He is . . . I dunno. Pretty much your basic human? He is always saying things like:

OH NO. -

WHAT NOW? -

SO TIRED. -

He doesn't have any lasers or rocket boosters or anything, but he is very good at hugs and also making sandwiches, and those are both IMPORTANT THINGS.

Anyway, the **EXCITED SWEARING** from her lab seemed like it was going to last for a while, so after a bit, Dad decided that maybe me and him and Alex should go for a little walk to the park.

"You have to understand," Dad said as we sat on a bench, "it means a lot to your mom, you guys going to that school. Making it work. She had to pull a lot of strings to get you there. Call in a lot of favors."

"Don't know why she bothered," I muttered super quietly, but apparently not quietly enough, because Dad gave me the **HARD STARE**.

"She bothered," Dad replied, "so that you'd have a chance to make friends, and have normal lives, and just . . . be people, and not spend your whole lives in a lab being monitored and tested and—and . . ."

And I think he must have run out of steam or, like, lost the use of language or something, because he just kind of threw his hands up and went "gahhh!"

"Hey, Dad?" said Alex. "Is it okay if we fly for a bit?"

"Fine," said Dad, taking a deep breath. "Don't go above four hundred feet, okay? I don't need you guys interfering with hover traffic."

And then he got, like, a haunted look in his eyes, and muttered "Not after the last time . . ."

"We'll be careful, promise," said Alex. And because Alex is so **GOOD** and **PERFECT** and has apparently **NEVER DONE ANYTHING WRONG**, that was good enough for Dad.

ALEX

Alex is my big brother. He is
always saying things like:

> FREDDY,
> NOT NOW.

> FREDDY,
> GO
> AWAY.

> FREDDY,
> STOP
> FOLLOWING
> ME.

Me and Alex are built from, like, the same designs,
except he is blue and lame-looking and I am bright
red and **AWESOME**. We go to the same school, but
I am under strict orders to . . .

★ Not **APPROACH** him at school.
★ Not TALK to or **EMBARRASS** him at school.
★ Not indicate that we **KNOW EACH OTHER IN
ANY WAY**.

If I try and talk to Alex at school, he acts confused and pretends we are not related. Which doesn't really work because we basically look exactly the same. And also, **WE ARE BOTH ROBOTS**. Which is a bit of a giveaway.

Alex started school years before I did, after we were adopted, when I was still just a baby. He was the first robot to ever go to school. And everyone always says how good he was, how he never caused any trouble or blew anything up with lasers or accidentally set fire to anything.

Anyway, with **GOOD AND SENSIBLE AND PERFECT** Alex supervising, we are sometimes allowed to fly at the park. We blasted off, and it was really nice to just fly. Just glide around and dive and swoop and do loop-the-loops and just . . . get up above everything.

After a while, Alex landed gently on the top of this really tall tree in the middle of the park. And I came down to join him, and we sat there in the branches, looking out over the park and the buildings, and the hover traffic drifting through the sky, and all the way across to the Mega-Skyscrapers over Canary Wharf.

"I know what it's like, Freddy," said Alex after a while. "I remember what it was like when I first started school. Mom never said this to me, exactly, but I could tell . . . a lot of people never wanted me to be there."

He paused for a minute, looking off into the distance. A bus drifted overhead.

"And it's hard. Because everyone treats you like you're this . . . social outsider," he continued. "And they're always watching you, every day. Watching and . . . waiting for you to mess up. Wanting you to mess up. Because if you mess up, you prove them right."

"Right about what?" I asked.

"That you're different," Alex said, watching a bird land on a nearby branch. "That you're not like them. That you're just . . . you know. A Dangerous Robot."

"But . . . you never got in trouble," I said. "Like, never. As I am always hearing. How did you do it?"

"You've just got to . . . try and keep your head down, you know? They're all watching you, so you just . . . don't give them anything to look at."

I thought about what that would be like. Not giving people anything to look at. Not being a celebrity or a superhero anymore.

Not being anything.

Honestly? I did not like the sound of it, **AT ALL**. But I didn't say anything.

"You can always blow off steam when you're back home," Alex continued. "Fire off your lasers, blow up some of the training droids at Mom's work. Come here and fly around. Just not at school, okay?"

"Okay," I said. "I get it."

"While you're there, you just keep quiet," Alex

continued. "Inconspicuous. You nod, you smile. You blend in. You don't give them an excuse."

"I can do that!"

Alex looked at me.

"Can you, though . . . ?" he asked.

"I can! I totally can!" I yelled, standing up on the branch and shaking my fists at the sky.

I CAN BE VERY QUIET AND IN-CON-SPICUOUS! !!!

But just then, the branch broke, and I fell out of the tree and landed in a garbage can, and it made a massive . . .

. . . and an old lady got all spooked and fell over into a hedge.

And okay, I admit, that was not a very good start.

CHAPTER
6

So all the next week at school, I was trying to do what Alex said and Keep My Head Down and Be Quiet And Inconspicuous, and stuff.

So it was one lunchtime that week that I ended up sitting next to . . .

Riyad.

I was still feeling a bit bad about Riyad.

"Hey. Um. Sorry," I said as I sat down. "About, y'know . . ."

Riyad didn't look up at me. We both looked down
at . . .

. . . his lunchbox.

Someone had put it back together with duct tape,
but it was still all bent out of shape, and I don't
think the lid closed properly anymore, and the
unicorns were all scuffed up so they still looked
like unicorns, but kind of Weird Broken Zombie
Unicorns.

"I was trying to help," I said. "And to **FIGHT
INJUSTICE** and stuff. But then, um, I sort of got
carried away, and everything got all mixed up, and . . .
anyway. Sorry."

Riyad just kept looking down at the lunchbox.

"I know that cartoon's for babies," he said, not meeting my eye. "But we watched it when I was little, and my mom . . . she doesn't get it . . ."

"Hey," I said to him. "Don't worry about it. I've still got some magic unicorn pajamas at home."

Riyad finally looked up at me. He even smiled, a bit.

"I mean, don't tell anyone. Obviously," I added quickly.

So I mostly ended up hanging out with Riyad that week. It actually turned out to be super fun, because he is really into **SCIENCE** and so he was very interested in, you know, me being an *AWESOME ROBOT*. We started doing a thing at lunchtimes called . . .

ROBOT RESEARCH

. . . where I would run him through a lot of the questions people always have about what it is like to be a robot and how we work and stuff. For instance . . .

*FREQUENTLY
ASKED
QUESTIONS!

(ABOUT
BEING A
ROBOT)

 Q: WHO BUILT YOU?

 A: Me and Alex were built by a genius mad scientist dude! I don't know very much about it, but **OBVIOUSLY** he was a genius, because he built ME.

 Q: DO YOU EAT FOOD?

 A: I **DO** eat food! Particularly food that is pizza!

 Q: WHY DO YOU NEED TO EAT FOOD? AREN'T YOU ROBOTS?

 A: **YES** but we are **VERY ADVANCED** robots. We eat regular food, and that gets turned into **FUEL** and materials for our robotic bodies! I can't remember how it works exactly, but the main point is, it is all **VERY CLEVER** and **HIGHLY SCIENTIFIC**.

Q: SO WAIT, DO YOU HAVE TO GO TO THE BATHROOM?

 A: I do NOT. This is **VERY UPSETTING**. Okay, so this is how my mom explained it to me.

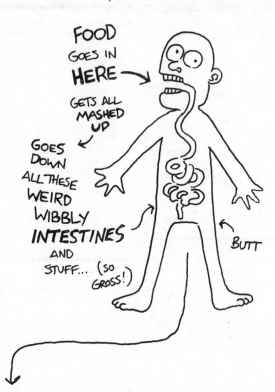

FOOD GOES IN **HERE**

GETS ALL MASHED UP

GOES DOWN ALL THESE WEIRD WIBBLY **INTESTINES** AND STUFF... (SO GROSS!)

BUTT

But then what's left over after all that, comes **OUT** of their bodies as **WASTE**.

Waste that comes out of their **BUTTS**.

LITERALLY OUT OF THEIR BUTTS.

THAT IS THE MOST AMAZING THING I EVER
HEARD, CAN YOU EVEN IMAGINE.

THEIR BUTTS.

Anyway, with me and Alex, on the other hand:

FOOD GOES IN **HERE**

GETS TURNED INTO ~ENERGY~ AND MATERIALS BY ~NANNY~ ~NINNY~ **NANO-TECHNOLOGY!**

REACTOR

. . . Because we are **HIGHLY SUPERIOR** robots,
the whole system is so efficient that **EVERY-THING** gets used up and there is no waste matter
left over at the end. Which is to say, there is **NO
POOP.**

I think this is basically just completely unfair.

I keep asking my dad what pooping is **LIKE** and trying to get him to **DESCRIBE** it to me, but he won't tell me anything useful. He just says that it's "not a very nice thing to talk about while he's trying to eat breakfast."

I just think it is **AMAZING** and **DISGUSTING** and **AMAZINGLY DISGUSTING**. Like, all humans do this! All the time! And they don't even THINK about how amazing it is. They are literally **PRODUCING SOMETHING OUT OF THEIR BODIES!** It is like a magic trick, except **SUPER DISGUSTING!** Or like giving birth to **BABIES**, which they seem to think is a pretty big deal, except even **MORE** amazing because they do this **EVERY DAY!**

Or, if they are my dad, **SEVERAL** times a day!

Riyad even had a bunch of LESS-frequently-asked-questions, about how our reactors work, and our onboard information systems, and stuff like that. To be honest, I didn't know the answers to most of them, but it was still nice to have an excuse to **TALK ABOUT MYSELF A LOT**.

And it was quite fun just to be able to, like, do robot stuff. The stupid CODE OF CONDUCT meant I wasn't allowed to use my lasers or rocket boosters or whatever, but as Riyad pointed out, I could still do lots of cool things that weren't in the CODE OF CONDUCT.

For instance, I borrowed the **Secret Robo-Communicator Watch** from Fernando so Riyad could try using it.

Apparently it has all these functions we've never even used, like Map References and Augmented Reality and stuff.

It even has a **HOMING FUNCTION**, where Riyad could make it send a signal and I would suddenly see these big blue floating arrows appear in the air that only I could see, pointing the way to the watch, wherever it was. It was like magic! We played **SECRET ROBO HIDE-AND-SEEK** to test it out, and by following the arrows, I could always find Riyad, even when he hid behind the **RECYCLING BINS**.

Anyway, all this was pretty fun, so I decided that Riyad should join the **S.O.**, which is a cool gang I started with Fernando and which **I AM THE LEADER OF**, whatever Fernando says. The one other member is Anisha, who always says she doesn't actually want to BE a member, but Fernando says it's not really a gang if you only have two members, so Anisha is a member **WHETHER SHE LIKES IT OR NOT**.

Anyway, I thought that since Riyad was so smart and good at science-y stuff he could join and be, like, our Science Officer. And Riyad said he didn't really know what that meant, but okay. And Anisha said great, you've got a new member, that means I can leave now, right? And Fernando said **NOBODY** leaves the **S.O.**

And Anisha said several rude words in Punjabi, but she hung around, which meant we had four members, which meant the **S.O.** was officially a **REAL GANG** now!

Which should have been great, but unfortunately . . .

. . . that was when things started to go a bit wrong.

All of us were out on the field—me, Fernando, Anisha, and Riyad, the whole **S.O.**—and Fernando was . . . being very Fernando, basically. My mom says that Fernando is "an Instigator." I think this means that he is always coming up with ideas that **DO** sound super fun, but it is often the kind of fun that ends up with me getting in trouble for blowing things up with lasers.

As well as being my Best Friend (Human), Fernando is also the **DEPUTY LEADER** of the S.O. He actually claims that HE started it and that therefore he is the Leader, but that is just ridiculous. Why would he be the Leader? He does not even have lasers or rocket boosters or super-strength or **ANYTHING**.

No one can really remember/agree on what S.O. stood for in the first place, so now we just change it to . . . whatever seems like most fun at the time?

★ Sometimes it stands for **SECURITY OFFICERS**, and we go around looking for Bad Trouble and **SPYING** on people.

★ Sometimes it stands for **SECRET ORGANIZATION**, and we are a cool Organized Crime Gang and we come up with **EVIL PLANS** and stuff.

★ One day it stood for **SANDWICH OBLITERATORS**, and we spent all lunchtime just straight-up destroying one another's sandwiches.

That last one was really fun, but then the egg salad

from Fernando's sandwich

accidentally went all over

the floor, and Mr. Latif

the P.E. teacher slipped on

it and twisted his ankle,

and that was pretty much

the end of the Sandwich

Obliterators.

Anyway, today we were all out on the field and Fernando had decided that today, **S.O.** stood for Stuntman Operations! Which basically just meant he was trying to persuade me to give him a Rocket Piggyback around the soccer field.

"I dunno, man," said Anisha. "I'm pretty sure Rocket Piggybacks are against the **CODE OF CONDUCT.**"

"Go on. Do iiiit," Fernando said.

Sometimes I think my mom is right about Fernando being an Instigator.

Riyad looked around nervously. "Who's on playground duty?" he asked.

"Miss Obasi," said Anisha. "But I just saw her go inside. I think she went to the bathroom again."

"It's all that coffee," said Fernando, and we all looked at one another sadly. It is a real problem.

"That gives us . . . three minutes," said Fernando. "Plenty of time."

I was tempted to just do it. Rocket Piggybacks **ARE** really fun, because **(A)** I get to fly **REALLY FAST** while Fernando hangs on to my back and tries not to fall off, and **(B)** I get to hear Fernando yell amusing rude words every time he thinks he is going to DIE.

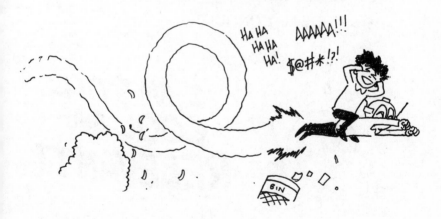

But no, I was trying to be **GOOD!** Now that I only had two strikes left, suddenly it didn't really seem like loads anymore? So I was really trying to stick to the CODE OF CONDUCT. And, frankly, Fernando was NOT HELPING.

I said to Riyad that maybe we should go off and do some more Robot Research together instead, and Fernando suddenly got really annoyed.

"Stop being BORING!" he yelled. "We used to do Rocket Piggybacks all the time! It is our thing!"

"Yeah, but I CAN'T now!" I yelled back. "I have a CODE OF CONDUCT, remember?"

"Ugh," said Fernando. "You are way more boring with a CODE OF CONDUCT."

"I am not boring!" I shouted.

I AM STILL COOL AND RELEVANT!

"Oh yeah?" said Fernando. "Prove it, then. I challenge you to . . ."

DARE-OFF DEATHMATCH !!!

"Um," said Riyad. "What does 'Dare-Off Deathmatch' mean?"

"Detentions for everyone, is what it usually means," said Anisha, although she looked **STRANGELY EXCITED** by this prospect.

"If I win, you give me a Rocket Piggyback!" said Fernando. "Three times around the field! If YOU win . . ."

And then he paused, because I don't think he had an idea for that.

But suddenly I had an idea.

"If I win," I said quickly, "then you agree that I am Permanent Leader of the **S.O.** For Life."

Because, I figured, if I was Permanent Leader For Life, then it wouldn't **MATTER** if I couldn't use my lasers or whatever, everyone would still have to be my friends anyway, because I would **LITERALLY BE IN CHARGE OF THEM**.

"You're on," Fernando said.

By now we had a bit of an audience. Even Henrik had skulked over to watch. He was muttering and acting like he was too cool to be there, but he WAS there, so there.

The first thing we did was to appoint Anisha as Official Dare-Off Deathmatch Adjudicator. "Ugh. Why do I always have to be in charge of this nonsense?" she said, even though we all know she secretly **LOVES BEING IN CHARGE OF THIS NONSENSE.**

Fernando shouted, **"SHOTGUN FIRST DARE!"** really fast, which wasn't FAIR because I wasn't **READY**. But Anisha said it still counted, and she is the official Dare-Off Deathmatch Adjudicator, so that was that.

"Nothing I'd have to use my powers for, though!" I said. "Just, like, stuff regular humans can do."

"Oh, that won't be a problem," said Fernando. And he actually **STEEPLED HIS FINGERS** like a baddy in a movie. "I dare you to run around the playground three times . . ."

"Is that it?" I asked. "That is barely even a dare!"

And then Fernando spun around and pointed at me like a full-on **SUPERVILLAIN**, and yelled . . .

...IN JUST YOUR UNDERWEAR!

CHAPTER 8

Everyone was gathered around watching me and Fernando, and at the word **"UNDERWEAR"** they suddenly all did a massive **GASP!** Like this was some big scary deal or something.

And I guess for most people—human people—maybe it would be. Apparently humans have this weird thing where they don't want other humans to see them in their underwear for some reason?

However, I am **NOT MOST PEOPLE!** I am an ***AWESOME ROBOT!*** And as far as I am concerned, the more people see of my awesome robot-ness, the **BETTER**.

Frankly, I would be quite happy to go to school **COMPLETELY NAKED**. I have actually suggested this to my dad, but he just looked tired and said something about a "uniform policy" and "being a part of society," whatever **THAT** is.

THE POINT IS: This was not a big problem for me.

I took all my clothes off in about ten seconds **FLAT** and handed them to Anisha.

"Hold THESE," I said.

"Absolutely **NOT**," said Anisha.

So I just put them on the ground. And off I went!

Lots of people had gathered around and were watching, but some people somehow hadn't noticed, so as I ran around, I made a point of yelling:

EVERYONE! CHECK IT OUT! I AM IN MY UNDERWEAR!

Fernando had **NO IDEA WHO HE WAS DEALING WITH.**

I did two laps around the playground and I would totally have done a third, but then Miss Obasi saw me and said, "Oh good lord, Freddy Sharma, go and put some pants on **THIS INSTANT.** Why do I even have to tell you these things?" And then her eye did like this weird **TWITCH** thing . . .

So I ran back to where everyone was and got a big round of applause. Even Fernando had to admit that I had **TOTALLY NAILED IT**.

"All right," I said as I put my pants back on. "My turn!"

I tried to think of something really good, something that Fernando would totally hate having to do. And then I had the perfect idea.

I copied Fernando's **Dramatic Pause, Turn, and Point** thing, because, honestly, it worked really well. And I said, "I dare you . . .

...TO EAT CABBAGE CUSTARD CURRY!

"Uh-oh," said Anisha.

Fernando went a bit pale.

"Um," said Riyad. "What is Cabbage Custard Curry?"

CABBAGE CUSTARD CURRY is a thing that I invented! You take . . .

★ One bowl of the school lunch Vegetarian Option **OKRA CURRY—** which is already pretty bad.

★ One bowl of the boiled cabbage that they force you to eat if you have the Roast Lunch Option.

★ One bowl of custard that you get for dessert.

And then **MIX THEM TOGETHER** to make . . .

Okay, yeah, it is basically what it sounds like.

Anisha's sister Jasminder is in the grade above us, and they were still having their lunches, so we got her to sneak out the **NECESSARY INGREDIENTS**. We mixed them all up . . .
and served it up.

I was pretty sure Fernando would admit defeat, because he is not even supposed to eat custard because he is a bit lactose intolerant and it makes him **SUPER FARTY**.

But he just narrowed his eyes at me, and picked up a spoon, and . . . .

. . . and I have to give it to him, he ate the **WHOLE BOWL**.

Also, it was cool how he **MAINTAINED EYE CONTACT** the whole way through. That was a pretty impressive move, even Henrik looked quite impressed by that.

When he was finished, he pushed the bowl away and he let out this absolutely **DISGUSTING**-smelling burp. He was clearly in some **INTERNAL DISTRESS**,

but he just grinned anyway and said it was my turn to do a dare.

"And I've got a good one for you," he said. "I dare you . . .

...TO DRINK TEN CANS OF GUNK!

And everyone who was watching did an even bigger **GASP!**

Because that was ludicrous.

CHAPTER 9

GUNK...

GUNK is this super-super-sweet sticky fizzy drink. We're not supposed to have it in school anymore, just because this goody-goody TV chef made a big deal about how it it is FULL of sugar and also **FULL** of chemicals, and also can **DISSOLVE BATTERIES**. But Fernando really loves it, so he smuggles cans of it into school inside his prosthetic leg. Which, honestly, is one of the coolest things I have ever seen a human do.

Everyone knows Fernando has a secret stash of cans hidden somewhere in the school, but he won't tell anyone where it is. It is, like, his most treasured possession in the world.

So the fact that he was prepared to give up **TEN CANS**, just to beat me in a Dare-Off Deathmatch, was frankly **RIDICULOUS**.

"Are you saying you can't do it?" asked Fernando, grinning.

"I could **TOTALLY** do it!" I yelled. "But it's not something a regular human could do! What would happen if you drank ten cans of Gunk?"

Riyad answered that one, in his official role as Science Officer.

"Um," he said. "I think if a human drank that much Gunk they would spend about an hour on the toilet. In agony. And also die."

"Awesome," said Fernando.

"So it's not fair!" I yelled.

"Is so fair!" yelled Fernando back. "You have to stick to your Robot Rules, right? Where does it say anything in there about fizzy drinks?"

We both appealed to Anisha as Dare-Off Deathmatch Adjudicator. From the side of the playground we were on, you could see though the windows to the cafeteria, where they'd put the dumb CODE OF CONDUCT up on the wall for everyone to see, so she read it out loud.

"No **SUPER-STRENGTH** . . . no **LASERS** . . . no **ROCKET BOOSTERS**," she read. "He's right. It doesn't say anything about fizzy drinks."

"But . . .

    but . . ."

I DECLARE IN FAVOR OF... **FERNANDO!**

YES!

WHAAAT!

Frankly, Anisha seemed to be enjoying this a bit too much.

Fernando grinned, ran off to his Secret Location, and came back five minutes later with his backpack bulging and clanking, and inside it . . .

TEN CANS OF GUNK.

He wasn't kidding.

Henrik, who had been hanging around sneering at everyone, skulked over. "Give me a can," he said to Fernando.

"No!" said Fernando. "We need it all for this!"

"**I SAID**," said Henrik, leaning right over Fernando, "give me a can."

"And I said **NO**."

Henrik just stood there glaring at Fernando for a second.

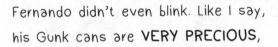

Fernando didn't even blink. Like I say, his Gunk cans are **VERY PRECIOUS,**

so he wasn't about to back down. And even though we were technically in the middle of a Dare-Off Deathmatch against each other, I went and stood behind Fernando to back him up, so we were like the . . .

ANTI-HENRIK LEAGUE

together.

And then Henrik made, like, an **ANNOYED GRUNTING SOUND**, and kicked a trash can over, and stomped off to the edge of the playground, where he continued watching us with a super-**EVIL GLARE**.

Anyway, everyone started yelling "Chug! Chug!" and so . . .

CHUG!

I **CHUGGED**.

See, it SHOULD have been fine. In theory, whatever I eat and drink gets processed by my highly efficient robot systems, so in **THEORY** I could drink Gunk **FOREVER**. It's just, drinking so much of it, all at once . . .

I guess it turns out my systems can only work so fast, because after about five cans, I really felt like I was starting to . . .

Fill up . . .

"Chug! Chug!" Everyone kept yelling. And the grin on Fernando's face was starting to slip a bit, because I made it through my sixth can . . .

And my seventh.

And my eighth.

But I wasn't feeling quite . . . right.

"You can give up any time you want," said Fernando as I cracked open the ninth can.

"NEVER!" I yelled, and downed it in one gulp. By this point, I was pretty sure I was going to short-circuit or melt or possibly explode. But if there's one thing Fernando should know about me, it is that I do **NOT LIKE TO LOSE.**

Thing is, neither does he. I was halfway through the **FINAL CAN**, and he could see I was going to finish it. So he ran over to me, and then turned around, and then let out the most enormous, disgusting, explosive . . .

**CABBAGE
CUSTARD
CURRY
FART!!!**

I swear, you could actually see it. It was like a giant toxic **FART MUSHROOM CLOUD**. It smelled like **EXPIRED MILK** and **CABBAGES** and **DEATH**.

I kind of laughed and hiccuped at the same time, and I think it gave me some kind of System Error. I felt all weird for a second, and then suddenly . . .

. . . it all came back up.

All ten gallons, or however much Gunk I'd drunk, just came **SPRAYING** out of me like someone had set off a **HOT STICKY BROWN FIRE EXTINGUISHER**, all over . . .

. . . Mr. Javid.

Who had just walked around the corner.

Which was unfortunate.

CHAPTER 10

So it turned out that **YES**, Mr. Javid was quite upset about being sprayed head to toe by an explosive **GUNK ERUPTION**. So that got put down as my **SECOND STRIKE**. My mom got called in to **YET ANOTHER** Meeting, and she tried to argue that it was an accident, and These Things Happen, and I hadn't technically broken the CODE OF CONDUCT rules.

And this was true! Technically. I tried to get Anisha to come in as Dare-Off Deathmatch Adjudicator to back me up. But Mr. Javid just said that Dare-Off Deathmatch Adjudicator was not in fact a legally binding title, and also that the matter was

NOT OPEN TO DEBATE.

So now I was on my **LAST LIFE**. And I hadn't even used my rocket boosters or lasers or **ANYTHING**. The whole thing was **SO UNFAIR!**

I was really angry with Fernando, for being a **JERK** and getting me my second strike. The whole thing was **HIS FAULT**, he absolutely **is** an Instigator, and honestly I thought **HE** should have gotten in trouble for the whole thing, not me.

But then Fernando actually **DID** get in trouble, too, for smuggling all the Gunk into school in the first place. **BOTH** his moms got called in for a meeting, which I guess must have meant **DOUBLE SCOLDING** when they got him home. He was grounded after school for a **WEEK** and had to spend every night cleaning his room and doing extra math homework.

So now Fernando was annoyed with **ME** for getting him in trouble. And I was annoyed with **HIM** for getting ME in trouble. Basically **EVERYONE WAS VERY ANNOYED WITH EACH OTHER.**

On Friday at lunch, me and Riyad were on Plate Duty. This is where you have to help the lunch ladies by collecting all the plates and cutlery from the cafeteria and taking them to the kitchens on these big carts, because Unpaid Child Labor is **TOTALLY FINE APPARENTLY** if you are a school.

Anyway, the point is, I was a bit late getting out to the playground. Which meant that by the time I got there, everyone had already started playing something without me.

Fernando and Anisha and even Henrik and everyone were all standing around in the corner of the playground, and they were playing . . .

SLAPSIES.

SLAPSIES!

A FUN GAME FOR ALL AGES!

HOW TO PLAY:

SLAPSIES is this game where one person holds their hands out, and then the other person tries to SLAP them as hard as they can. The first person has to try and move their hands away in time.

But if they're not quick enough . . .

KA-SLAPPP!!!

THEY GET SLAPPED.

It is super funny to watch, because the people who get slapped are always crying and screaming and leaping up and down shouting rude words. Apparently being slapped hurts quite a lot, and yet for some reason they all want to keep playing it?

I wouldn't know, because I am **NOT ALLOWED TO PLAY**, just because my hands are made of **INDESTRUCTIBLE HEAVY METALS** or whatever, and if I played, I could "literally break someone's fingers."

But Fernando said, sorry, it was already decided, today S.O. stood for the **SLAPSIES OLYMPICS**, and they couldn't stop now because Henrik and Arjun from the other class were already having the semifinals.

They had decided what S.O. stood for without me!

Just then, Anisha, who was apparently being Official Slap Referee, ruled that Arjun had **FLINCHED** and therefore Henrik got a free slap.

I think it is pretty unfair that they would all play a game that **(A)** I am not allowed to join in with and **(B) LOOKS SO FUN**. And so I told Fernando and all of them this **VERY LOUDLY**.

Fernando agreed that okay, **YES**, maybe it was **SLIGHTLY** unfair, but I was late getting there after Plate Duty, and also it was just too much fun **NOT** to play. And right then, Henrik slapped Arjun really hard, and Arjun's hand went bright red, and he yelled what my translation software informed me is a **REALLY** rude word in Punjabi, and everyone laughed, and it was **SO UNFAIR**.

"Well, if you're all playing **THIS**, maybe me and Riyad will go and do some Rocket Piggybacks on the field instead!" I said to Fernando. Which made Riyad look really panicky, but I didn't really mean it, I was just trying to annoy Fernando.

"Fine! Go, then!" said Fernando, **DEFINITELY** annoyed. "We'll just keep playing our **AWESOME GAME WITHOUT YOU.**"

And suddenly I could just see that this was what it was going to be like now, with the stupid CODE OF CONDUCT. If I couldn't use my lasers and rocket boosters and everything . . . if I couldn't give them a show . . . everyone was going to forget about me. I wouldn't be a celebrity **OR** a superhero anymore. I'd just be left out, getting pointed at and whispered about and having to stand around and watch while they all did **FUN HUMAN STUFF** together.

HUMANS (JERKS)

I did **NOT LIKE** this idea. I might not be a celebrity anymore, but I was still Leader of the **S.O.**, so I told Fernando that I was **ORDERING** them to stop all the slapping and play something I could join in with instead.

"Pretty messed up, letting a robot boss you around like that," muttered Henrik.

"Shut up, Henrik," said Fernando. But still, he wouldn't budge and said they were going to finish their game.

"But . . . it was an **S.O. ORDER!**" I said. "You are **DISOBEYING A DIRECT ORDER!**"

"You can't give me orders, Freddy," said Fernando, looking really annoyed. "You're not my boss."

In the background, Henrik gave an annoying snicker.
But Fernando and I just stood there glaring at each
other.

I was really angry now.

And Fernando was really angry, too.

And that . . . was when it all kicked off.

CHAPTER 11

"You are being so annoying!" I shouted.

"YOU are being annoying!" Fernando shouted back.

"Good points, both of you," said Anisha. "But maybe we should all just stop shouting?"

"HE STARTED IT!" me and Fernando both yelled at the same time.

"I **TOLD** you I can't play this game," I continued, frustrated, "and you are doing it anyway!"

"Yeah, well, you don't always get to be in **CHARGE** of everything!" said Fernando.

"I am the Leader of the S.O.!" I shouted, feeling **INCREDIBLY FRUSTRATED**. "What is the point of even having human sidekicks if they don't do what you say?"

And Fernando got a funny look on his face.

"Did you just call me a human sidekick?" Fernando asked.

"Yes!" I said. "That is how it works, remember? I am the Leader of the **S.O.** and you are my sidekick! But not a very good one, frankly!"

"I'm the Leader! I started it," he shouted.

"I started it!" I corrected him. Also shouting.

"Um. Maybe we should change the subject?" said Riyad, nervously.

"Obviously I'm the Leader!" I shouted. "I am an **AWESOME ROBOT!** I have rocket boosters and lasers and super-strength and everything! What have you got? Nothing! You're just . . . . a **HUMAN!**"

"Yeah?" Fernando shouted back. "At least I am a human!"

And then everyone went very quiet. And I think there must have been, like, a gust of wind and some grit went into my ocular receptors or something, because my eyes were suddenly stinging. But I

WASN'T CRYING. Because everyone knows, crying is the **NUMBER ONE** Thing You Just Don't Do.

So I definitely, absolutely, positively was **NOT** crying.

I just want to be clear about that.

I shouted at Fernando that he was an idiot and that he was banned from the **S.O.** forever! And he shouted back he didn't even **CARE**, because he was going to start his **OWN** secret organization called the **X.O.** that would be even **BETTER** and that I wasn't allowed to join. And I shouted that I wouldn't **WANT** to join, it sounded ridiculous, what did the X even **STAND** for? And he shouted it didn't **MATTER** what it stood for, it was just **COOL**.

"Fine!" I said. "Go! I don't care! Good luck coming up with words that start with X!"

"That's it," Fernando yelled. "Come on, Anisha, we're leaving!"

I yelled back "Anisha, do **NOT** go with him. That is an **ORDER!**"

And then we looked around and realized that Anisha had already walked off.

Riyad was standing there, and he looked all nervous and said, "Um. She said . . . Um, well, she said she was going to play field hockey, because you are both being . . ."

We glared at him.

". . . well, um, what she actually said was a bit rude."

He looked very embarrassed.
"Sorry," said Riyad.

And then Fernando stomped off in one direction . . .

. . . and I stomped off in the other direction, and that was that. It was the **END OF THE S.O.** . . .

FOREVER???

CHAPTER 12

After that, things were pretty quiet at school. Anisha went off with her Field Hockey Club friends, and Riyad went off with his Science Club friends, and who even cares what Fernando was doing, he was a **JERK**. So it ended up that I had no one to sit with at lunch or play with at recess.

I was all on my own. Which meant, as my mom puts it, that I had a lot of time to Think and Reflect on My Actions.

If there is one thing I really hate, it is Thinking and Reflecting on My Actions. It is **THE WORST**.

So instead I passed the time daydreaming about a list of my . . .

 TOP **5** THINGS I WOULD DO IF I WAS AN EVIL ROBOT WHO ENSLAVED HUMANITY

1) MAKE EVERYONE WEAR UNIFORMS

Just so they all look stupid, basically. Just the stupidest-looking uniforms you can imagine.

2) MORE HOMEWORK

Not for **ME**. In this daydream, I am an evil robot who enslaved humanity. Obviously I don't have to do homework. But **LOTS**, for everyone else. Especially **STUPID FERNANDO**.

3) NO MORE UNETHICAL TREATMENT OF THE ELEPHANTS

People are way too mean to elephants, and elephants are awesome, so in my New World Order, anyone who attempts to Treat an Elephant Unethically will be **ZAPPED WITH LASERS.**

4) BROCCOLI TO BE OUTLAWED

(Self-explanatory.)

5) EVERYONE TO BUILD A CASTLE FOR ME TO LIVE IN, WITH MY FACE ON IT

A really **BIG** castle, with lots of room for me and my Army of Ethically Treated Elephants.

This was such a fun thing to daydream about that it almost made me forget that I was sitting at a table all on my own and didn't have any friends anymore and that everything was **TERRIBLE** and **STUPID**.

But then someone **DID** come over to my table. I looked up because I thought maybe it was Fernando coming to apologize and beg to be let back into the **S.O.**

I was already thinking about whether I would allow this, and what **TESTS OF ALLEGIANCE** I would force him to do, when I noticed that it wasn't actually Fernando at all.

It was **HENRIK**.

"All right, Robot," he said.

And he sat down.

So I ended up mostly hanging out with Henrik at school that week. I know, I'm as surprised as you are. But if the choice was hanging out with Henrik or being all on my own, then I guess I was going to choose Henrik.

And actually, Henrik was being weirdly okay with me. He didn't punch me, he didn't shove me. There wasn't even that much rudeness. We just kind of . . . hung out. I don't know if it is because he knew I wasn't allowed to use my lasers now, so he had decided I wasn't a threat? Or maybe, underneath it all, he was just actually sort of . . . nice? Like maybe he was one of those people you see in movies, who seem like they're all mean and scary on the outside, but then you get to know them and they turn out to be all soft and cuddly on the inside.

And then I saw him punch a kid in the grade below and steal his sandwiches . . .

. . . and I thought, okay, maybe not soft and cuddly, exactly.

But the main point was that I had someone to hang out with at recess and lunch, and Fernando didn't, which meant I was **TOTALLY WINNING**.

In class that week, we were working on our new project, which is all about . . .

LIFE UNDER THE SEA.

We're going to be studying it all semester, and at the end of semester, we're going on a school trip to this awesome massive aquarium place in the middle of London called the **FISHTANK**. We all got put into groups, and each group has to study a different sea creature and make a **DISPLAY** about them, and the group that does the best display wins a **PRIZE**.

Anisha and Riyad got to be in the group that was studying sharks, which looked really cool. And Fernando was in a group that got to do giant octopuses, which looked really cool, **TOO**. But I got paired up with Henrik, and we got stuck learning about . . .

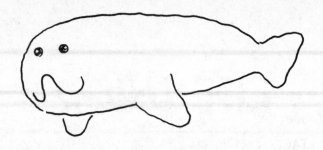

. . . manatees.

MANATEES. Literally all week. Over and over, the same stuff, until I got so bored of manatees I thought my brain was going to **ACTUALLY PHYSICALLY MELT.** Here are my

 **FACTS ABOUT MANATEES:**

1 There is nothing interesting about manatees.

2 What even are they? They are like **OVERWEIGHT DOLPHINS.**

3 They live in the sea, which is also home to a lot of **MUCH COOLER ANIMALS.**

4 For example: **SHARKS.**

5 . . . **THAT'S IT.**

We all had to make these massive papier-mâché sculptures of the creatures we'd been learning about. And it was really unfair because Fernando's group got to make this awesome 3D giant octopus, and use chicken wire to make these great big twisty **TENTACLES** for it, and it just looked really **COOL**.

Whereas our manatee . . .

. . . well.

It basically looked like a **MASSIVE WET POOP**.

I think Henrik used too much water in the papier-mâché.

Miss Obasi asked for volunteers to help hang everyone's models up in the gym, to make a big display for our Project Outcome Evening. I put my hand up, but she just looked at me and said, "Ah, not you, Freddy." They took all the other groups' models to be part of the display, but they decided not to use ours. Apparently it "looked structurally unsound." So everyone else went off to hang up their models, and me and Henrik just sat there with our Sad Poop Manatee.

And I was so annoyed, and just so bored of manatees generally, that I kind of snapped. I looked at the stupid model sitting there, looking terrible, and just yelled at it:

I HATE YOU, MANATEE!!

And then it was weird, suddenly Miss Obasi looked really nervous, and I got pulled out of class and had to go and sit in a little room by myself and talk to the school counselor. She got out this big folder about "safeguarding procedures" and "radicalization," and they were even talking about calling the **POLICE** in and it was all just getting really **WEIRD**. I thought this was going to be it, and this would be my last strike and I was going to get expelled, and I didn't even know what I'd done.

Anyway, eventually it turned out Miss Obasi thought I said "I HATE HUMANITY," which was why she got so nervous. But I DIDN'T, I said "I HATE YOU, MANATEE!" The whole thing was an Unfortunate Misunderstanding.

So they let me go back to class, and I wasn't expelled, and it was like I got an **EXTRA LIFE**. So I guess everything was fine?

But it was all a bit exhausting. And when I got back to class, there was **LOTS** of pointing and whispering and giggling going on.

1-UP!

And I'll be honest. I was starting to get a bit fed up.

It felt like I couldn't do anything right. Like even when I was really trying, I kept messing up, and half the time I didn't even know what I'd done.

You know when you are playing a video game and you get to a really hard part and whatever you do you just keep dying and eventually you just get so annoyed that you . . .

RAGE QUIT!

. . . and then Dad scolds you and you're banned from playing video games for a **WEEK?**

School . . . was starting to feel like that.

CHAPTER 14

The next week, we had an assembly where Mr. Javid gave this big speech about our Project Outcome Evening and how it is this massive huge deal. Everyone's parents and guardians were coming in to see all our work, and there would be **PRIZES**, and also we would have some **SPECIAL GUESTS**. Everyone got excited because we all thought maybe that meant someone from TV, but no. It is just some "Local Business Leaders," apparently.

I asked my dad later what Local Business Leaders are, and it turns out it basically just means People with Money. Dad guessed Mr. Javid was probably trying to hit them up for some sponsorship cash to finally replace the school hover-bus, because the one we've got is super old and a bit beat-up and smells like several people have puked in it. Mainly because several people have puked in it.

Anyway, after the assembly, me and Henrik got told to stay behind, and Mr. Javid came to have a **TALK** with us. He said that there's a lot riding on this, so you two in particular are to be on your **BEST BEHAVIOR**, is that understood?
And we both said, "Yes, Mr. Javid."

But I looked over at Henrik.

And he was grinning.

That afternoon, we had to go home from school and then come **BACK** to school in the evening, and that **ALWAYS** feels weird. You know those nightmares you have where you're being chased by giant disembodied sets of **HUMAN TEETH?**

And then you wake up and you think it's all over?

But then the **TEETH ALL JUMP OUT FROM UNDER YOUR BED** and you realize you are **STILL IN THE NIGHTMARE?**

It is like that.

Mom and Dad came along, and all the parents made a big show of oohing and aahing at the big display in the gym. Everyone's Life Under the Sea models were hanging from the ceiling, and they'd

done this cool thing with the lights so it looked like
the models were all actually swimming around under
the sea.

Except for our manatee, which was put over in a
corner on its own, and no one was looking at it,
except occasionally a parent would sort of notice it
by mistake and then do a little jump
and quickly back away looking
WORRIED and **SAD**.

All the kids in our year were being **HOSTS** and **GUIDES**, Meeting and Greeting the parents and the Local Business Leaders and answering all their questions about the school or marine habitats or whatever.

All the kids except for me and Henrik, anyway. We had been told to stand in a Designated Area in the corner, next to our Sad Poop Manatee. Mr. Javid had been very specific about this, he said it was important for people to see us there, to "demonstrate the school's Commitment to Diversity," but that under **NO** circumstances were we to actually talk to anyone or do anything or move from our Designated Area **AT ALL**.

It was **VERY BORING**.

On the wall near us was a big poster of the Fishtank, where we'll finally get to go at the end of the semester. Alex got to go there when he was in our grade and I was **SO JEALOUS**, it sounds amazing. There are all kinds of different sea creatures there, and also a cafe that makes hot dogs, but the main point is: They have **SHARKS!** So having to just stand there all night was **SUPER BORING**, but I just stared at the poster, and thought about getting to go and see the sharks, and tried to get through it like that.

Once everyone had been Met and Gret, they all went and sat down in front of the stage to have the

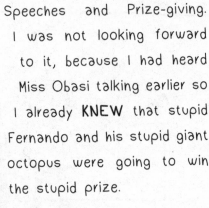

Speeches and Prize-giving. I was not looking forward to it, because I had heard Miss Obasi talking earlier so I already **KNEW** that stupid Fernando and his stupid giant octopus were going to win the stupid prize.

We snuck around the corner, in the dark, into the parking

lot. And we kept going until we got to the far corner. And there, Henrik ducked behind one of the parked cars, and pulled out something he had stashed there.

"Look what I found," Henrik said. It was this big plastic box, like one of those fridge boxes you take on a picnic. "Hidden at the back of the P.E. storage room, under the gym mats . . ."

And he opened it up.

My eyes boggled a bit, because I couldn't believe what I was seeing.

"Is that . . . ?"

And it was.

It was **FERNANDO'S SECRET GUNK STASH!**

"This is great!" I said. "Let's drink them all!

"Or wait, no," I added, because I remembered what had happened the last time. "Let's just throw them all away. Fernando'll be so annoyed when he finds out . . ."

But Henrik said, "Oh no. We're not just going to throw them away. We're going to do something much better than that."

And he grinned again, and said:

"I've got a plan . . ."

CHAPTER

So Henrik explained his plan. It was a pretty simple plan, which was that we would take Fernando's cans of Gunk . . .

And we would blow them up with lasers.

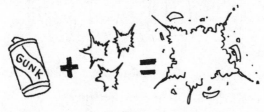

"Come on," he said. "It'll be fun."

And it did sound fun. It sounded really, really fun. **BUT** . . .

. . . I knew I wasn't supposed to. It says right there in the CODE OF CONDUCT: NO LASERS.

BUT . . .

. . . there wasn't anyone around to even **SEE.** All the teachers were inside the school.

I looked over to check. Through the window, I could see them all. And Mr. Javid, giving the prize for Best Model. Of course, he was giving it to . . .

Fernando. Standing there all happy, smiling and joking with all the other humans in his group, all his fellow winners. And all the way from where we were, I could hear them all laughing. And then it was faint, but I was sure I just heard the word "Manatee," and then all of them laughing again.

I could feel my lasers getting all hot and itchy, and I could have just fired them up and blown up their stupid octopus right there and then, rules or no rules.

"Imagine his face." Henrik grinned. "When he goes to his precious Gunk stash, and finds them all **BLOWN TO PIECES**."

And that **WAS** fun to imagine.

"But . . . the CODE OF CONDUCT . . ." I said.

"Forget the stupid CODE OF CONDUCT," said Henrik, giving one of the Gunk cans a shake. "Don't you want to see what happens when one of these **EXPLODES?**"

And you know what? I did want to see that. I wanted to see that **SO BAD**.

We went around the back of the science block because Henrik said he knew a spot where no one would be able to see what we were up to.

He got out one of the cans and said "Ready . . . get set . . ."

FIRE!

I **AIMED**,
and I **FIRED**,

and . . .

KA-SPLOW!!

. . . it was amazing.

The can completely **EXPLODED** into, like, a radioactive
sugary chemical MUSHROOM CLOUD.

So obviously we had to do another one immediately. This time Henrik really shook it up beforehand, for extra explosiveness. And then . . .

Henrik grabbed another can and gave it a massive shake. And he said to get ready, because this one was going to be something **REALLY SPECIAL**.

KA-SPLOOGE!!

"Ready . . . get set . . ."

And he threw it farther than ever! Right toward the science block!

It was going so fast, I had to do my very best aim, and . . .

I hit it! And there was the BIGGEST *EXPLOSION* SO FAR.

KA- SPLODE!!

But also, this time, suddenly the air was filled with this incredibly loud

"What is **THAT?**" I asked. "It sounds like a **FIRE ALARM** going off!"

And Henrik started laughing his head off. "It IS the fire alarm! Ha ha ha ha! I don't believe it! You totally **BLEW UP THE FIRE ALARM!!**"

And I had! Henrik had thrown the can right in front of one of the fire alarm sensors, and I had accidentally set it off with my lasers!

And I had a horrible feeling suddenly. Because if the fire alarms were going off, that meant . . .

I was in serious trouble.

CHAPTER 16

The alarms were still blaring, and I felt all sick and panicky as I ran away from Henrik and back to to the gym as fast as I could. And when I got there, I saw . . .

AWOOGA! AWOOGA! AWOOGA!

All the sprinklers in the gym were going off! Everyone was getting soaked—all the kids, all the parents and teachers, all the Local Business Leaders. Everyone!

But that wasn't even the worst part.

Everyone's papier-mâché sea creatures were soaking up all the water from the sprinklers . . .

. . . getting all
SOGGY and **SLIMY**
and **HEAVY**, until . . .

They started to fall.

A big **WHALE** was the first to drop. It hit the floor with a massive

and soggy papier-mâché slime went all over one of the Local Business Leaders. Then another fell. And another!

It was like a **WET SLIMY UNDERWATER NIGHTMARE!** Everybody was starting to **PANIC!**

Mr. Javid was soaking wet, but he was trying to yell at everyone to **STAY CALM** and **NOT FREAK OUT** and **FORM AN ORDERLY LINE TO EXIT**.

But just then . . .

. . . the octopus dropped.

I could barely even look. I kind of just peeked through my fingers and saw . . .

Mr. Javid standing there, with the big soggy octopus plonked right on his head. He looked like some terrible half-man, half-octopus creature or **SOGGY ANCIENT GOD.**

And he just raised his fists to the sky, and shouted:

. . . just assuming it was all my fault, again.

I mean, okay, it **was** all my fault again. But still.

I considered my options and decided that the best thing to do at this point, basically, was to get very far away, as quickly as possible.

But as I turned to try and sneak out of the door, that's when I bumped into . . .

Mom.

CHAPTER 17: FUN INTERACTIVE QUIZ!

What do **YOU** think happened next?

★ If you think Freddy's mom said, "Oh, that's fine, these things happen, don't worry about it," and took him out for **ICE CREAM** . . .

GO TO OPTION A

★ If you think Freddy's mom was SUPER ANGRY and all the teachers were SUPER ANGRY and basically EVERYONE IN THE WORLD WAS SUPER ANGRY . . .

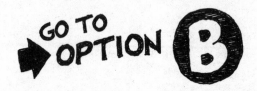

GO TO OPTION B

OPTION

Are you even serious? Ha! Enjoy living in your **HAPPY DREAM WORLD**, you **SAP**. No! Go back to the start and choose again!

OPTION B

YES.
OBVIOUSLY
THAT IS
WHAT
HAPPENED.

Everyone knew it was me that had shot the fire alarm with lasers. Which wasn't hard, because I am the only one at our school who has lasers.

But the really unfair part was that Henrik pretended the whole thing was my fault! He told the teachers that I'd just run off and started shooting lasers, and that he had nothing to do with it. Even though the whole thing was **HIS PLAN!**

I don't think the teachers really trusted Henrik. But it was his word against mine, and they **DEFINITELY** didn't trust me, so it looked like he was actually going to get away with it.

When we got home, I could tell Mom was really angry. But she didn't shout or get upset or anything, she just went **SUPER QUIET** and went off and shut herself up in her workshop.

SLAM!

I thought she must have left it to Dad to do all the shouting. But then HE didn't get upset, either. He made me a hot chocolate, and then we sat at the table and Had a Talk while Alex lay on the sofa playing video games.

I asked if I was going to get expelled, and Dad said he didn't know, but maybe. I asked where I would go to school now, and Dad said he didn't know that, either. It might be that I didn't get to go to school anymore and they'd just have to figure something out where I had classes on my own at Mom's work or something.

And still no one was shouting at me, and it was starting to make me feel really **WEIRD**.

I thought about never going to school ever again. And even though that is a thing I have daydreamed about on a daily basis for literally **EVER**, the idea of it actually happening was much less fun. Suddenly getting out of Math Jail didn't matter at all anymore. All that mattered was that I'd lost all my friends, and now I'd probably never see them again. And I felt all weird and cold and my chest hurt and I wondered if maybe my reactor was malfunctioning or something.

Dad said that he knew it must be difficult at school sometimes. Fitting in, when you're different from everyone else. Or when everyone thinks you're different, anyway.

He said it's a tough thing, and no one can really do it for you, you just have to figure it out for yourself the best you can.

And maybe some people cope by doing everything they can to blend in, and not make any noise, and kind of slip under the radar.

And maybe other people cope by going the other way, and making as much noise as possible, and basically blowing everything up with lasers.

And he said that it would be nice if I could stop blowing things up with lasers **QUITE SO MUCH**, but also that I was still learning this stuff for myself, and he thought maybe sometimes everyone forgot that a bit.

And then he just gave me a hug, and did a sort of sad smile, and went off to start making dinner.

I just sat there. After a bit, Alex looked over at me.

"You all right?" he asked.

And I didn't really have an answer for that.

"You want to have a fight for a bit?" he asked. "Shoot some lasers at each other or something?"

And it was weird, because usually that is **LITERALLY ALL I WANT**, but today I just wasn't in the mood.

Alex looked at me and then gestured to the gamebox with his controller. ". . . or we could just play something together?"

"Mmph," I said.

"You can pick the game," Alex said.

". . . Fine," I said.

So we just sat there on the sofa and played video games together for a while.

We ended up having a good long session of . . .

STREETS OF FIGHTING!

It is one of my favorite games, but Alex usually won't play it with me because he says it is "repetitive" and "unimaginative" and "horrifyingly violent."

But today he played it with me. And we punched and kicked and fought off literally **HUNDREDS** of

Street Punks, and we got all the way to level twenty, and we defeated the Boss Punk together and everything! It was the first time we'd ever managed to do that, and I set a new high score for "Punks Defeated"!

It was so awesome that for a second . . .

I forgot that everything was terrible.

CHAPTER 18

LUNCHBOX INCIDENT
GUNK INCIDENT
OCTOPUS INCIDENT

GAME OVER

I mean, I still got expelled. Obviously.

Mom and Dad went in and had a meeting with Mr. Javid, but Mr. Javid wouldn't budge. I'd had my Three Strikes, and now there was No Other Option. Dad said Mr. Javid was just annoyed because the Local Business Leaders had been scared off and now he wasn't going to score that sweet Sponsorship Money for a new school hover-bus. But either way, that was that. I had to stay at home while Mom and Dad Made Other Arrangements. I didn't get to go back to school, ever. And I didn't get to go on the Fishtank trip.

And the worst part was, I couldn't even enjoy sitting around at home because I felt all horrible and bad about everything that had happened. Not going to school meant I had nothing **BUT** time to Think and Reflect on My Actions and, as I might have mentioned before, **I DO NOT ENJOY THAT**.

I kept going back and forth. I spent half the time just feeling awful and blaming myself. For ruining the Project Outcome Evening, and destroying everyone's models, and blowing up Fernando's Gunk stash and everything. For using my lasers when I knew I wasn't supposed to.

And the really bad part was that I knew that I hadn't done it to fight injustice. I hadn't even done it to show off. I'd done it because I thought it would hurt Fernando.

And knowing that didn't make me feel very good at all.

Anyway, I didn't like feeling that way, so I spent the other half of the time feeling angry with everyone else.

With Mr. Javid, for always having it out for me. With Henrik, for getting me to do it, and blaming me for everything, and getting me expelled. And with Fernando, whose fault it probably all was in the first place, for reasons I couldn't exactly remember, but I knew I was still **VERY ANGRY** with him.

With all of them. All of the stupid humans and all their stupid rules and their stupid . . . complications.

 I declared loudly.

"Well, you can make your own sandwich, then," said my dad, and he put the bread down and left the kitchen.

"I didn't mean **YOU!**" I shouted after him.

Anyway, just then, someone knocked at the door, and Dad yelled at me to get it because he was in the bathroom. And I thought it was probably just the mailman or something. But it wasn't the mailman.

Standing there on the doorstep were Anisha and . . .

Fernando.

CHAPTER

"Hey," I said.

"Hey," said Fernando.

And then we just sort of stood there for a bit.

"Oh, for . . ." said Anisha. "Fernando, didn't you have something you wanted to say to Freddy?"

Fernando looked down and sort of kicked at the pavement.

"Mblsmsl," he mumbled.

"What?" I asked.

"I'm sorry," he said.

"What?" I asked, again. Because honestly, I wasn't sure what was happening.

And then I heard the toilet flushing, so I invited Fernando and Anisha to come in, and we went into the living room before my dad came along, because he would probably have **QUESTIONS**.

When we got there, Fernando saw the game that me and Alex had been playing, and immediately his eyes lit up. "Aw sweet, you have **STREETS OF FIGHTING!**" he said. "Can I play?"

"Fernando!" said Anisha. "You were in the middle of **SAYING** something?"

"Oh, yeah," said Fernando, looking annoyed. "Um . . ."

And then we just stood there for a bit. And then he finally said: "Stinks about you getting expelled and stuff."

"Yeah," I said.

And then we just stood there for a bit again.

"**AND** . . . ?" said Anisha, shoving Fernando.

"And, **OKAY,** I'm **SORRY,**" Fernando continued. "I'm sorry about what I said and stuff."

"I'm sorry," I said. "About what I said and stuff."

"I didn't mean you weren't a real person," said Fernando. "I was just angry . . ."

"I didn't mean you were a human sidekick," I said, looking at the floor. "I was just angry . . ."

And then it all started pouring out, and apparently somehow there was a gust of wind inside our house because I think I must have got a bit of grit in my ocular receptors again.

"I was just . . ." mumbled Fernando, kicking at the floor. ". . . I thought . . . you didn't want to be friends anymore. You were always hanging out with Riyad instead, and doing your Robot Research together or whatever . . . and then you took back the **Secret Robo-Communicator Watch** and gave it to him . . ."

The watch! I'd forgotten all about that.

". . . and you never gave it back. And . . . that was always our thing . . ." said Fernando, still kicking the floor.

"I didn't give it to him, I just borrowed it back!" I said. "It's upstairs in my room. I just forgot! I thought you didn't want to be friends anymore!"

"What?" said Fernando.

"I thought . . ." I started. ". . . if I couldn't give you Rocket Piggybacks, or use my lasers and stuff . . . you wouldn't want to hang out with me anymore."

And Fernando just gave me a look.

"Freddy . . ." he said, "I don't hang out with you because you have rocket boosters or lasers or whatever. I hang out with you because you're funny and awesome and you're my best friend."

And then . . . it all got a bit emotional.

"I think I preferred the awkward silences," said Anisha.

So me and Fernando pulled ourselves together, and I went and grabbed the **Secret Robo-Communicator Watch** from my room and gave it back to Fernando. We were officially **BEST FRIENDS** again, and we even made up a special new **S.O. SECRET HANDSHAKE** to celebrate!

Anisha just said a couple of mild swears and muttered something about ". . . boys and all your DRAMA."

Anyway, after that, Anisha fired up the gamebox and we all played *Streets of Fighting* together for a bit. It was super fun because we could play three-player, which lets you do some really cool **TEAM COMBO TAKEDOWNS.**

And also Dad brought us some sandwiches!

"I am sorry, though," I said after we finished taking down a gang of Street Punks. "About the thing with the sprinklers. Ruining your models and everything."

"Are you kidding me?" said Fernando. "That was amazing!"

"Did you see the octopus land on Mr. Javid?" said Anisha. "I nearly peed myself."

And then they both did impressions of Mr. Javid with the octopus on his head, going . . .

FREDDY SHARMAAAAA

. . . and we all laughed.

"And then he finally managed to get it off," said Anisha, grinning. "And chucked it . . ."

"... right into a couple of stampeding Local Business Leaders!" added Fernando.

"And then one of them got their feet all tangled up in its tentacles . . ."

"... and they tripped over and totally faceplanted . . ."

"... right into your Sad Poop Manatee!" they both finished together, and fell over laughing.

And that did sound pretty entertaining, I had to admit.

"It was literally the greatest thing that has ever happened in school," said Anisha, wiping away a tear from laughing so much.

"I do wish you hadn't blown up my Gunk stash, though," said Fernando. "Like, I'm not mad. I just didn't know you even knew where it was."

"Yeah," said Anisha. "Like, I get that you were annoyed with Fernando. He is very annoying . . ."

"Hey!" said Fernando.

"But," continued Anisha, "you could have just talked to him, instead of, y'know . . . blowing everything up."

"No . . . I . . ." I said, because I was confused. And then I realized, they didn't even know what had really happened.

"I didn't . . . it wasn't my idea!" I said. "It was Henrik!"

And I told them the whole thing, about how he'd come up with the plan, and got me to blow up the fire alarm, and then lied to the teachers and blamed me for everything.

"Wait. Are you saying he planned the whole thing?" said Anisha. "He wanted to get you expelled?"

"Of course he did!" I yelled. "He's always had it out for me! He is . . . he is like an evil genius!"

"Henrik . . . is an evil genius? Henrik?" said Anisha, and she really didn't look very convinced.

"We can't let him get away with it!" said Fernando. "It is . . . it is **INJUSTICE!**"

I **AGREED**.

"If it was his plan . . . and we could **PROVE** it was him," said Anisha, looking thoughtful, "then Freddy would be in the clear . . ."

". . . and he could come back to school!" said Fernando.

And suddenly my chest didn't feel all weird and cold anymore, it was like someone had flipped a switch. Because suddenly there was **HOPE**. And I know, it's weird. I never thought I'd be so excited by the thought of going back to school. But I really, really was.

"But how would we do it?" said Anisha. "Prove it?"

Fernando paced around the room, muttering. "Ugh. Henrik's got all the teachers fooled. He is so slippery, he is like an eel, or . . .

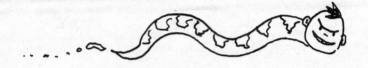

"Wait," he said. And he suddenly got a real Fernando Look in his eyes.

"I just had the best idea."

CHAPTER 20

So it was about a week later. I was still off school, just . . . sitting around in my pajamas eating chips, basically. Which, I admit, sounds pretty fun, but was actually **SURPRISINGLY BORING**. I had spent the morning trying to persuade my dad to play Atomic Robo-Ball with me, which was a **FUN NEW GAME** I had invented. But he just kept saying he was "trying to work," and that it was "difficult to concentrate over all the explosions," it was very frustrating. But just then, my antennae started pinging—there was a call coming through on the **Secret Robo-Communicator Watch!**

171

Which must mean . . . it was time.

"I'm just going up to my room for a bit!" I yelled at my dad, who just sort of gave a relieved sigh.

As soon as I got to my room, I answered the call, and Fernando and Anisha popped up on my screen.

"Operation Undercover Eel is **GO**," said Fernando, grinning.

"Where are you guys?" I asked. "Are you . . . ?"

"Yeah—check it out!" said Anisha. And she must have, like, grabbed Fernando's wrist and pointed the watch around, because the picture on my screen moved. I could see rows of seats, and Riyad sitting behind them, and Henrik two rows back, and everyone from our class. They were all on the hover-bus!

"Look!" said Anisha. "We're here!"

And Fernando held the watch up to the window so I could see . . .

The whole of London, spread out beneath them.
Lines of big red hover-buses and Skytube trails criss-
crossing the sky. The river, bright in the sunlight.
And right ahead of them, shining like a beacon . . .
the Fishtank!

The Fishtank is . . . possibly the coolest place in the entire universe? It's right by the Thames in the middle of the city, next to the old London Eye. And it's like twenty stories high, and the entire sides of the building are made of glass, and the whole thing is filled with water, so it's basically one massive skyscraper-sized aquarium. People walking past and people flying by in cars and buses can all see the fish swimming around, all the way up. It is so cool. It looks like they are swimming in the SKY.

So **PHASE ONE** of our plan was just sneaking me along on the trip so I didn't have to miss out. Even though I wasn't actually there, and I was just seeing the whole thing on a screen in my head via Fernando's **Secret Robo-Communicator Watch**, it was like I was there, and that was still pretty cool.

The hover-bus landed in the parking lot on top of the building, and then, of course, there was this whole delay when half of the kids in the class needed to go to the bathroom immediately. Me and Fernando both got super alert at that, because if Henrik needed to pee then that might be our chance to put **PHASE TWO** into action. But he didn't need to go, so we had to wait.

But that was okay, because in the meantime, I had a **FUN UNDERCOVER SCHOOL TRIP** to go on. First, this tour guide started showing everyone around. They got to go on these cool walkways that go all around the outside of the building so you can look in at all the fish. There were whales and eels and manta rays and all sorts of awesome weird fish I don't even know the names of.

Fernando would hold the watch out so I could see everything, and occasionally Miss Obasi would get suspicious and ask what was going on, but Fernando just said he was "pointing out features of scientific interest."

And then Fernando held me right up against the glass and whispered, "Freddy, check it out, there they are." And there they were. Drifting toward us through the dark water. The **SHARKS**.

I am **SUPER** into sharks. I have a whole book about them at home called **SHARK FACTS**. When I was little, I would sit and read it for hours, to the point where my dad said it was getting "a bit disturbing." Basically, sharks are **COMPLETELY AMAZING** and I am slightly **OBSESSED** with them.

For example, **DID YOU KNOW** that great white sharks can smell blood from **MILES** away? Like, even just a tiny drop of blood in the water and they'll be straight on the case like, "Oh, What Is That Over There? Is That a Human Who's Cut Their Finger or Whatever? Hey, Here's an Idea: Let's Go And **KILL AND EAT THEM.**"

Also, humans are totally **TERRIFIED** of them for some reason. It is very entertaining!

Anyway, at the Fishtank they only had **TIGER SHARKS**, not great white sharks, which are my **ABSOLUTE** favorite. But they were still **AMAZING**. The way they just glide around, so quiet and so serene and so **AWESOMELY DEADLY**. At one point, one swam

right up to the glass in front of Fernando. He held
me up to it on his watch, and I could see right
into its **BLACK SOULLESS MURDERER'S EYES,** and
honestly it was one of the most amazing moments
of my life.

And then before you knew it, it was time to go.
First, there was another trip to the bathroom. And
this time Henrik **DID** need to go.

"Phase two is **GO**," whispered Fernando.

And he followed Henrik . . .

into the bathroom.

CHAPTER 21

I switched the **Secret Robo-Communicator Watch** to MUTE so I could hear what they were saying, but no one could hear me, so Henrik couldn't tell I was there. And Fernando was using this other function on the watch that Riyad had showed us how to work, where it could **RECORD** everything people were saying. It was very exciting as I watched on the screen as Fernando followed Henrik in. It was like being on an **UNDERCOVER BATHROOM MISSION**.

Although apparently Henrik is very quick at going to the bathroom, because by the time Fernando got in, he was already on his way back out toward the door. Fernando stepped in front of him, blocking his way.

"Out of my way," said Henrik.

"No," said Fernando. "I want to have a **WORD** with you."

"Oh yeah?" said Henrik. "About what?"

"About how it was **YOUR** idea to steal my cans of Gunk and blow them up! And about how you tricked Freddy into shooting the fire alarm!"

Henrik just narrowed his eyes and looked at Fernando. "Don't know what you're talking about," he said.

"You DO know!" said Fernando. "Admit it, the whole thing was your plan!"

"What plan? What are you talking about?" asked Henrik.

"It was all a **PLAN** to get Freddy expelled," Fernando continued, starting to shout now. "And it is all **YOUR FAULT,** and you should totally **CONFESS!"**

"Psst! Play it cool!" I whispered to Fernando. But then I remembered I was on mute, and he couldn't hear me.

And I think Fernando was a bit overexcited, because he started getting upset and waving the watch right in Henrik's face and yelling, "Confess! **CONFESS!"**

Which was maybe not exactly playing it cool.

Henrik said, "What are you up to?" And he grabbed Fernando's wrist and pointed at the watch. "What's this, huh?"

"Ow!" said Fernando. "Get off!"

"Are you trying to record me?" said Henrik. "What is this, like, your secret plan?"

I couldn't just watch anymore, so I took myself off mute, and I popped up on the screen there with them. **"YES,** it is a secret plan!" I yelled at Henrik. "Now, get off him and confess!"

"Don't know what you're talking about," said Henrik again.

"You are being such a **JERK!**" I yelled at him. "Just **ADMIT** it was all your fault!"

"Or what?" said Henrik. "What are you going to do about it?"

"We'll . . ." said Fernando.

"We'll . . ." I said.

And then we just looked at each other because, honestly, we didn't really have a plan past this point. Henrik was supposed to have confessed already.

Okay, look, maybe our plan could have used a bit more planning.

"Yeah, you've got nothing on me," said Henrik. "But now I've got something on you. If you ever mess with me again . . ."

And he kind of poked Fernando in the chest.

POKE!

"I'm going to go and tell the teachers that you and your little robot friend go around trying to secretly record people in the bathroom."

And okay, sure, when you put it like that, it didn't sound very good.

"You are such a jerk!" yelled Fernando. "Why are you always picking on people?"

And Henrik spun around like a **MANIAC** and **PUNCHED** one of the paper towel dispensers right off the wall!

"**YOU** can talk!" he yelled. "You two! With your best friends and your little gang! Why are **YOU** always picking on ME?"

And he stomped out of the room, giving the broken paper towel dispenser a kick on the way out and slamming the door behind him.

Me and Fernando just looked at each other, confused. We weren't picking on Henrik. That was ridiculous.

Wasn't it?

Anyway, there wasn't really time to think about it, because everyone had to get back on the bus. Henrik was still stomping around like a lunatic, and as he got on, he gave the side of the bus a massive **KICK**.

"How did it go?" Anisha asked us. And neither Fernando or me really wanted to get into details, but we had to admit that it had **NOT GONE VERY WELL**.

"So that's it?" asked Riyad. "Freddy's not going to be coming back to school?"

"We'll think of something else," said Anisha.

"Tell you what," said Fernando into the watch, "we'll all come over on Saturday and come up with a new plan, okay? Even if you're not at school, we can still hang out on Saturdays."

"Yeah," said Anisha. "S.O. can stand for . . . Saturdays Organization now."

And I could see the three of them on my screen, Fernando, Anisha, and Riyad. My friends, smiling at me.

And I thought, Saturdays Organization. Maybe that wouldn't be so bad.

When suddenly there was huge

The picture on my screen lurched. And I heard someone scream, "We're falling!"

"We're falling out of the sky!"

Everyone on the bus started to panic, and I couldn't really see anything because everyone was all crammed together and panicking and my watch was all pressed up against what I think was Riyad's **BUTT**.

I could just hear Miss Obasi trying to talk:

"Everyone, listen. The antigrav field generator must have burned out! Just calm down!"

Unfortunately lots of people did **NOT** calm down, but instead started freaking out and saying how they were all going to **FALL TO THEIR DEATHS**. There was quite a lot of screaming, and Miss Obasi shouted for quiet.

It was weird, because usually at school she is all jittery and nervous, but now that there was an **ACTUAL LIFE-THREATENING EMERGENCY,** she was suddenly like Super In-Charge Woman.

"Everyone, **STOP SCREAMING and LISTEN,**" said Miss Obasi. "Hover-buses are statistically a very safe form of transport, and it is **INCREDIBLY** rare for even one antigrav generator to stop working. And even if it did, it's still perfectly safe, there are still three backup generators to get us safely back to land. We're going to be **FINE**."

And then there was another **BANG!**

"Miss?" asked Riyad. "Was that one of the backup generators?"

And then there was another **BANG!**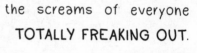

"Um," said Miss Obasi.

And then there was another

BANG!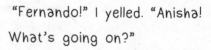

And then the picture on my screen went really blurry, and I could just hear the screams of everyone **TOTALLY FREAKING OUT.**

"Fernando!" I yelled. "Anisha! What's going on?"

But then the picture went blank. I could just hear someone—I think Riyad?—yelling "Quick! Give it to me, I'll send a—"

And then the whole thing cut out.

CHAPTER 23

~~XXX~~

My screen had gone dead, and suddenly I was just back on my own, in my bedroom, with my chips. And I didn't know what to do!

I had to go help them, go save everybody! I ran down the stairs and out the front door, but then I just stopped. There in the street, in my pajamas. Because

I didn't know where to go.

I know the way to the corner store, and to school, pretty much, but . . . I wasn't sure which way to go to get to the Fishtank. That was miles away. And they could all be crashing to the ground right now, and I was just standing there like an idiot, and I couldn't do anything.

Then, suddenly, my antennae started pinging again. But it wasn't a call, it was . . .

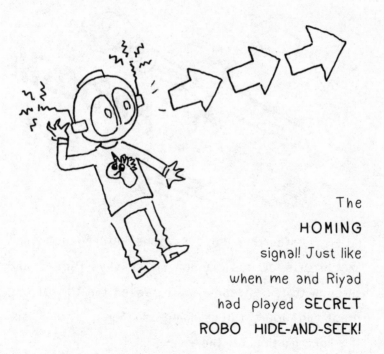

The **HOMING** signal! Just like when me and Riyad had played **SECRET ROBO HIDE-AND-SEEK!**

Suddenly I could see, like, these blue arrows in the sky, showing me exactly where to go—showing the way . . . to the communicator watch! To where Fernando and Anisha and Riyad and all of them were!

Where they were in trouble, and they needed me!

I flew, faster than I'd ever gone before—following the arrows across London, past skyscrapers and through traffic streams. As I passed the top of one great big apartment building, suddenly I could see the light glinting on the river . . .

And then the arrows veered off to the left, over
the river and across the top of Waterloo Station,
all the way to . . .

The Fishtank!

And there, near the top of it . . .

The hover-bus! It had fallen against the side of
the building, and there were tiny cracks spreading
out across the glass from where it'd hit. It was
hanging there all tangled up in the steel walkways
that crisscrossed the side of the building. I used my

OPTICAL ZOOM and I could see everyone there, inside the bus, pressed up against the windows. There was Fernando! And Anisha! And Riyad and Miss Obasi and Henrik and everyone! They were safe!

Well, they were safe. But just then, the steel walkways that were holding the bus up suddenly snapped, and the bus gave way . . .

. . . and started plummeting toward the ground.

CHAPTER 24

I could see all these terrified humans on the ground, pointing and starting to run away. But they'd never get away in time—the bus was falling so fast!

I flicked off my boosters for a second, so I started to fall, too. And I let myself fall, stretching my arms out ahead of me, so I was diving headfirst, straight down.

And then I fired the boosters back up again, **MAXIMUM POWER**. I zoomed forward, falling faster than gravity, faster than anything, racing the bus down through the sky, until just as we were about to hit the ground . . .

I beat it! I passed it! I twisted around, facing back toward it, stretched out my hands . . .

And grabbed it! Just flipping **GRABBED** the front of the bus, as hard as I could. The metal went all **SCRUNCHED UP** in my hands, my fingers digging in like it was modeling clay. And then I fired up my rocket boosters again at **FULL POWER**, and I shouted . . .

We were so close to the ground, I think my rocket boosters might have scorched the pavement, and possibly a couple of people's cars, and possibly a couple of people. But it worked! I gripped on as tightly as I could, and the bus wasn't falling anymore. I was holding the whole thing up!

It was super heavy. It was a whole **BUS**, full of people! But, as I may have mentioned . . .

I am an *AWESOME ROBOT*.

I slowwwly powered down my rocket boosters, drifting downward, carefully lowering the bus, and set it down on the ground.

And there was this massive cheer from inside! Everyone was okay!

I mean, mostly okay. There were a few bumped heads and black eyes, and it smelled like maybe there had been a few more bus pukes in all the excitement. But everyone had all their arms and legs still on, and no one had **DIED HORRIBLY**, so all in all, I thought that was a pretty good job.

Miss Obasi had gone a bit pale and was shaking. I asked her if she was okay, but she just held on to my hand really tight until we had got everyone off the bus and made sure no one was hurt, and then she just kind of dropped down next to me and gave me a massive hug.

Fernando and Anisha ran over to us.

"Freddy, that was amazing!" said Anisha. "You saved everyone!"

"You are like a flipping **SUPERHERO**," said Fernando.

"I AM like a flipping superhero," I agreed.

And I struck my best . . .

AWESOME SUPERHERO POSE

. . . right there on the pavement.

I think it would have looked pretty dramatic if it wasn't for the fact I was still in my pajamas.

"Freddy," said Fernando, "you know how we would totally be friends with you even if you didn't have lasers and rocket boosters, right?"

"I know," I said.

"But I have to say," Fernando continued, "the fact that you **DO** have lasers and rocket boosters . . . **DOES NOT STINK.**"

And we gave each other our special **S.O.** Secret Handshake.

But just then, someone cried out, "**LOOK!**"

He was pointing up at the Fishtank, at this spot about halfway up. There were all these lines spreading out across the glass, from where the bus had hit it. And there was this horrible spreading crunching sound. And suddenly I realized: The glass was splintering.

The whole thing was going to crack open.

CHAPTER 25

There was a giant **KRACKKKK!!**

And a massive **SPLOOOSH!!**

And the side of the Fishtank just **SHATTERED**.
A great spout of water came pouring out!
It was like someone had turned on a

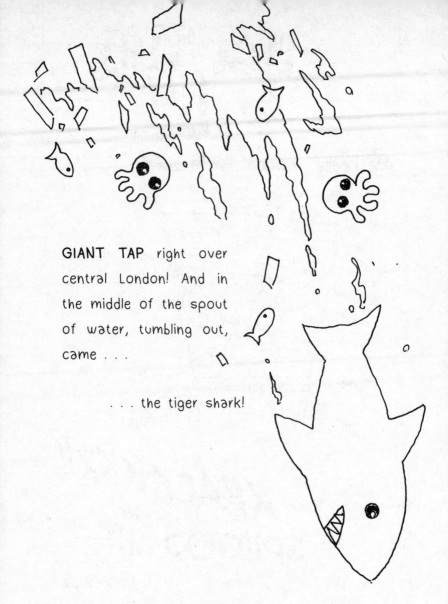

GIANT TAP right over
central London! And in
the middle of the spout
of water, tumbling out,
came . . .

. . . the tiger shark!

Falling out of the sky, straight down, like a giant
ANGRY FISH MISSILE! Right toward . . .

Henrik!

Despite the fact there was a shark falling out of the sky toward him at a hundred miles per hour, Henrik wasn't running away.

He just stood there frozen, his eyes bulging out with this look of absolute confused terror, like . . .

. . . well, pretty much like a very large shark was falling out of the sky toward him at a hundred miles an hour, I suppose.

For a second, I thought about just **LETTING** the shark fall on him. Because, frankly, if anyone deserved to have a shark fall on them at a hundred miles an hour, it was Henrik.

But only for a second.

"Do it." Fernando grinned.

So I did. I fired up my **_ROCKET BOOSTERS_** as hard as I could, and flew straight toward it, and . . .

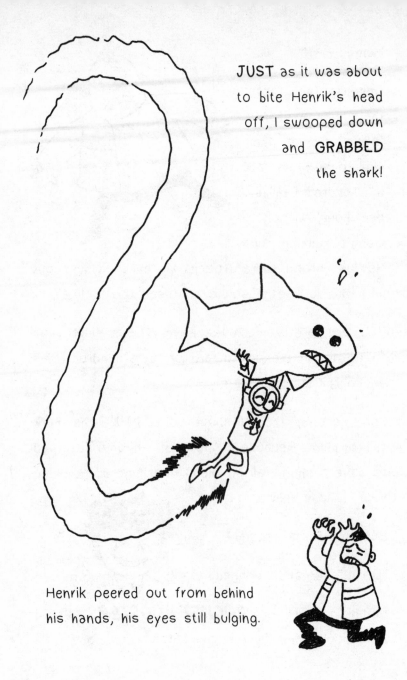

JUST as it was about to bite Henrik's head off, I swooped down and **GRABBED** the shark!

Henrik peered out from behind his hands, his eyes still bulging.

"Wh-what happened?" he asked.

"Oh, hey, Henrik," I said. "What's up?"

And then Henrik went
very pale and
fell over . . .

THUNK!

. . . and I went off to find the shark some water.

CHAPTER 26

After that, things got pretty busy!

First, Alex turned up! He said that it had been on
the news at school that there was an Incident at
the Fishtank, and that he figured "Incident" probably
meant me. Which I found a bit offensive, but okay,
fine, he was actually right, so whatever.

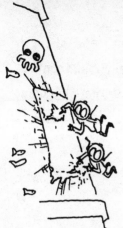

Anyway, he helped me get the shark back inside, and then we **SEALED UP** the side of the Fishtank, welding it back shut with our Mega Robo Lasers. It was pretty cool.

Also:

★ The **POLICE** came.

★ The **FIRE DEPARTMENT** came.

★ A whole bunch of **AMBULANCES** came.

★ Even a couple of **R.A.I.D.*** vans from Mom's work came!

* (**R.A.I.D.** stands for Robotics Analysis, Intelligence, and Defense! I got my mom to write it down.)

And my mom was in one of the vans, and she ran over and gave me a massive **HUG**, right in front of everyone, and told me how proud of me she was, and it was kind of embarrassing, but also secretly quite nice.

Anyway, between them all, they managed to get the side of the Fishtank properly secured, and everything was **OKAY**. Even the tiger shark was okay! Despite all the excitement, once he was back in the water, he just kind of happily swam off looking for something new to murder, it was **PRETTY ADORABLE**.

And then we all got to ride back to school in police hover-vans! And when we got there, Miss Obasi told everyone how I'd saved them all, and made me stand up and take a bow, and everyone clapped and cheered and it was just **AWESOME**. It was like being a celebrity **AND** a superhero, all rolled into one! Except even better, because I was with all my friends and they were all celebrity superheroes, too!

And Alex hung around and was smiling and joking and letting people see us together and didn't even pretend we weren't related or **ANYTHING**.

Oh, also, Henrik was okay, too. He came around in a minute or two, and they gave him some hot chocolate and took him off for a nice sit-down, and he seems fine now. I mean, every now and then his eyes will bulge out madly and he will wave his arms around and yell . . .

THE SHARK!
THE SHARK!!

But apart from that, he is basically fine. And I guess he was actually quite affected by the whole thing, because he went to Mr. Javid and **CONFESSED!** He told him how it was his idea to blow up the Gunk cans, and how apparently he didn't mean for the fire alarm to get exploded, that was just an accident. It hadn't been a whole Evil Plan to get me expelled . . . he just thought it would be funny to blow up the Gunk cans. And I guess I couldn't really argue with that because . . . I had thought it would be funny, too? And when it all went wrong, he'd just blamed me so he wouldn't get in trouble himself. And I guess I couldn't really argue with that, either, because . . . I'd blamed him, too?

It is annoying when you want someone to be an evil genius and they turn out to just be a person like you.

Anyway, the point is: I am not expelled anymore! After Henrik's **DRAMATIC CONFESSION**, Mom had another meeting with Mr. Javid. Dad and Alex went in to argue with him, too, and Anisha started a whole **PETITION** and everything. As she pointed out when she handed it in, it was actually quite a **GOOD** thing having a superpowered robot around the place, and if I hadn't been expelled in the first place, I would have been right there on the spot to help, and they wouldn't have had to do all that **NEARLY FALLING TO THEIR DEATHS**. And Miss Obasi looked directly at Mr. Javid and said: "You know what? She's right."

So in light of the fact that **I LITERALLY SAVED EVERYBODY'S LIVES**, and also a rare marine animal, Mr. Javid finally gave in! So now I get to come back to school after all! I get to stay with all my friends!

But also, I still have to do math.

So, again, bit of a mixed bag, really.

The dumb Robot Rules are still up in the school cafeteria, but Dad got them to add an asterisk, so now it says:

ROBOTIC CODE OF CONDUCT

USE OF SUPERHUMAN ROBOTIC ABILITIES IS STRICTLY FORBIDDEN ON SCHOOL GROUNDS.

NO SUPER-STRENGTH

NO LASERS

NO ROCKET BOOSTERS

***EXCEPT** IN THE CASE OF LIFE-THREATENING EMERGENCY

Which is something, I suppose.

3-UP!!!

And I have three whole new strikes! Miss Obasi said I should get to "start again with a clean slate." It is awesome, it is like getting a whole bunch of new lives! And this time, I am going to be **SUPER GOOD** and **WELL BEHAVED** and there won't be **ANY MORE INCIDENTS**, probably.

The one sad thing is that the poor old (smelly) hover-bus didn't make it. The whole thing was totaled and it got towed away for scrap. But the good news is, Mom talked with her bosses at **R.A.I.D.** and they donated . . .

A BRAND-NEW state-of-the-art hover-bus! With the latest ultra-stable antigrav field technology! And it doesn't smell of vomit or anything! So Mr. Javid is happy, because that is one less thing the school has to pay for, I guess? Also Mom said she'd souped it up a bit with anti-crash force field generators and some concealed defensive missile systems, "just in case."

Did I mention that my mom is pretty cool?

Also, the **S.O.** is re-formed! Me and Fernando agreed to **COMBINE OUR FORCES** once more, and we are not even arguing over who gets to be Leader anymore.

Anisha said she was tired of our nonsense and had decided that **RIYAD** should be the new Leader, and even Fernando agreed. Because apparently Riyad was amazing when the bus engines exploded; he was **SUPER CALM** and knew exactly what to do, and sent me the map code straightaway while everyone else was still busy panicking and yelling about how they were all going to die.

So we decided that since he had shown such Excellent Leadership Skills, Riyad could be in charge for a while! And be official Leader and get to decide what we do at recess and what **S.O.** stands for and **EVERYTHING**.

And then Riyad started to look all panicky and worried. He said it was a lot of responsibility and there were so many factors to consider, and he couldn't decide if we should be the Science Organization or the Secret Oligarchy or the Subaquatic Operatives or . . .

And it looked like this might go on for a while. Just then, I saw Henrik skulking around the edge of the playground, all on his own. And for some reason,  I suddenly thought of what Alex had said. Ages ago, back at the park. About how hard it can be when you are a social outsider.

And I suddenly thought, maybe that is what **S.O.** could stand for. Maybe we could all be Social Outsiders together. And maybe that would make it easier for all of us.

I mean, obviously, I didn't actually say all that out

loud because I thought it would probably so
SUPER LAME. I just said, "Hey, why don't we all
play catch for a bit? And hey, maybe Henrik would
like to join in?"

So that is what we all did. And it was pretty fun!
We just threw the ball around and laughed and
shouted, and Henrik didn't even punch anybody or
anything. And I thought, you know what, I actually
am glad to be back at school. Because it might be
boring and terrible and basically **MATH JAIL**. But it
is where my friends are. And my friends are pretty
great.

I mean, you know.

For humans.

THE END

About the Author

Neill Cameron is an award-winning writer and cartoonist. He is the creator of several comic books, including **MEGA ROBO BROS** and **HOW TO MAKE AWESOME COMICS**. Freddy vs. School is his first novel.